G R JORDAN

The Demon's Chalice

Dark Wen #2

To John,
always a better friend than I,
but with a rather poor taste in Gridiron teams!

Contents

Chapter 1

In case you don't know me, I find a particular solace in my coffee. So much so, that I am sat outside when the air temperature is cold enough for jackets and gloves. And just to drink my coffee with the sounds of the city at my favourite little beverage house. You see my mind is troubled.

Only a few months ago a dark entity rolled into town and I was involved in preventing its followers from blowing many people to kingdom come, but not before it had destroyed several lives, including that of my previous boss. It also, via a woman with a pair of the most evil eyes I have ever seen, paralysed the legs of my new partner. And I'm also a few fingers down because of it. But the worst was the fact that my friend, a nun with no eyes, wasn't able to stop the manifestation of the actual *Darkness* coming. That's the name of the entity, The Darkness.

So we have been waiting for a few months, waiting for its next move. I've been tasked by my new Chief, the view of the suicide of the last one is still too damn fresh in my mind, with seeking out this *Darkness*, protecting the city from it. But because that's weird, I'm simply running a department called *Special Detachments*. Or as the precinct boys and girls call it, the freak squad.

Ah, here's Karen with my coffee. She's looking at me as if I'm deranged, sat at an outside table when there's snow on the ground. I smile and give her no reason to doubt that assumption. The black steaming mug of liquid causes a misty vapour to rise above it and I see her look out along the street. Karen's thin, but not ill looking. She suits her elegant figure and she's a lovely image to accompany my coffee. Also a clever girl, a student at the university, earning enough to get by at this establishment.

"It's all gone quiet, Detective Trimble, there's so little heard about it now. It's like the city's back to normal."

After the incidents surrounding the evil presence arriving (that's a mass bombing, a suicide bomber, a poisonous gas release and a ship full of explosives, not to mention a ton of other shit before that), the city was kind of nervous. But they don't know the real issue. The dark demons that came, the things that made the so called horrible stuff seem almost light. That was the real issue. The people never saw a dead body rise and then take itself along to an incinerator. I bloody did.

"It will come back, Karen, evil doesn't stay quiet for long. That's why I'm still in a job. And it's Kyle. None of that detective bollocks."

"Of course, Officer."

I take the joke in good humour and watch her turn around and go back inside. She's a lovely sight, trim and with soft hair. I don't mind who serves my coffee but as a man, when it comes from the hand of a sweet woman, it's never bad.

It's late in the afternoon and the city is getting ready for rush hour. I endure the stares of people walking past, checking out the lunatic at the outside table. The sky is darkening and more snow seems to be on its way.

"Hey, what sort of an ass sits outside on a day like this?" The voice is a woman's and one I recognise very well. I turn my head and see the long dark hair of my partner, Detective Kyla Corstain, wheeling herself along. What's she doing out of the apartment on so cold a day? She's meant to be recovering after she was paralysed.

"Hey, what's the crisis?"

"Do I need a crisis to come and see my friend? Knew you'd be here."

"No you didn't," I laugh, "You rang the station. It's a hike to here across city traffic, whereas the station is just along from the bus route. You rang!"

"Always the detective."

"Well it takes one to know one."

She wheels herself to my little alcove, a sight I'm trying to get used to. In case you don't know, she's more than a partner. The young woman, fifteen years my junior has blown me away. During the previous turmoil, we kinda almost got it on. I guess in a lot of ways we did. But then she was suddenly wheelchair bound.

Yeah, I know, a person who can't use their legs is still a person like anyone else and we shouldn't treat them any different. I have done my diversity training. But they don't train you for this sort of shit. I mean, she's struggling with it. Some nights she has cried on me for over an hour. Maybe it's what happened and things we saw. Maybe it's just "these bloody legs".

But the other thing is the way it changes how we interact. At first, she needed lots of help. Although it's not fitted out for someone in a wheelchair, Kyla still insisted on living at my flat. And for a few weeks I was helping her change, bathe and getting her in and out of bed. Whereas before I'm taking in every view of her, simply enjoying any raunchy moments we have, now I'm almost feeling like it's wrong to enjoy her body, because she's struggling to choose what I see and don't see.

"Mulgrew, are we going to the recital tonight? I mean you haven't come up with another way to get out of it?"

I laugh at her directness but it's an accurate statement. Neither of us really like classical music that much but she needed to start getting out and about so I got us tickets. She's even got a new dress for the occasion and when I saw it, I knew it was for my benefit. Or maybe she was just trying to prove to herself, that she can be as hot and sassy as the next woman despite being on wheels.

That's the mobile. She's going to freak if this is a job. And the timing of it. Damn unreal.

"Yeah, it's Trimble."

Kyle Mulgrew Trimble in case you were wondering at all the names, Irish in background, total dogged bastard of a policeman.

"The City museum? Why...? If it's just a robbery, why me...? The Chief wants me." I see Kyla roll her eyes. Trust me, girl, I've seen the dress and I want my classical music. "Okay, if he wants me then I'll be there... But there's no one dead...? And he wants me...? Okay, twenty minutes."

"You are unreal, I knew it wasn't going to happen."

I look at her in the tight leather jacket and warm gloves she's got on, topped with a bobble hat. But my mind sees the diving neckline and the trace of her chest, her long brushed hair framing a stunning face and a night of promise.

"Get your wheels in motion, you're still a policewoman. Let's grab a cab, get over there, get it done and get out of there. We have a date!"

Chapter 2

The City museum is an old building designed by someone who decided to forget everything he had learned at architectural college, everything about how building's work and what looks good in a place where people hang out, and instead build an unworkable monstrosity in order to get his name in lights. As I can't remember his name, it didn't really work.

Thankfully legislation has meant the museum has had to adapt to the idea that all people should be able to use the building so there are a number of fix-its in place for those less mobile or with other requirements beyond that of an aging detective. It does mean I have to wait at times as Kyla wheels herself off round some improvised ramp but I'm just glad she's out and about. It wasn't so good during the first month after the incident.

Speaking of which, the first officer I meet in the building is Kobold, hero of the hour when the Darkness tried to blow up the dam and flood a football stadium in order to kill many people. She's still very green but she's got something about her. When the dust had settled I asked her to join my department. As she obviously didn't want a proper career, she said yes.

"What's the deal, Kobold?"

"Well boss, there's been a theft from the reserved collection, the ones not on show to the public. If you'll follow me as you may not have been in this part of the museum before."

This part? I've barely seen anywhere in it. Think I popped in for a toilet stop once. When it comes to the history of this world, I prefer a docudrama. Although I've fallen asleep in most of those.

Kobold takes us through to a storeroom in the rear of the building, deep in the recesses. There are a plethora of metal racks, all with boxes which are stamped with a code. As we move down one of the aisles, I see Jenny Tatler, scenes of crime expert, once a lover of mine, and thankfully still a very good friend. For a woman missing an arm, she hasn't let it stop her. Clever, resourceful and the better of me.

"Jenny, how's my favourite scenes of crime hottie."

Jenny looks down at Kyla in her wheelchair. "You okay with him hitting on other women?"

"If we don't get out of here in time for the concert, he won't have anything left to impress other women with."

"Go girl," laughs Jenny. "Good to see you on the move Kyla, you can't let these things stop you. Okay, we have a strange one here. One package opened, one item taken, nothing else in the warehouse touched."

"There's only basic security in this part, boss," says Kobold. "Nothing in here is particularly expensive in monetary terms, if it was, it would be in the vault just along from here."

"And yet I have a clean job, Trimble. This particular aisle hasn't been walked on for at least a week. Apparently it is rare that these items get worked with and then it tends to be when collections are changed over in the display cabinets."

"When you say clean, no fingerprints, no footprints? I mean

there's dust here."

"I think Jenny knows clean, Mulgrew."

Magic, I hate it when women gang up on you. But this is strange, very strange. If the place was a mess, it might have been a random grab.

"What's missing then?" I ask.

"It's a minor piece from a Haitian collection. Described as a chalice, a type of cup, wooden and pretty plain. It's only got a few markings on the side."

"Photo?"

"No sir."

"Kobold, how many times, it's Trimble. You saved all our lives up on the dam. It's Trimble, you're part of my team now."

"Yes sir... sorry, Trimble."

"What were the markings?"

"They were very basic, I'll go get the curator in charge, as I think he'll have the best idea." Kobold walks off and I hope she can get this boss / colleague relationship thing. I might be the lead but out here we all back each other as friends.

"Trimble, take a look at the box it was in," says Jenny, pointing with her only hand. "It wasn't opened with a knife. Considering how clean everything else is, you'd expect a clean cut with a sharp knife to gain entry. But instead it's a tear."

"Like something tore at it with its mouth," chirps Kyla.

"Mouth?" I query.

"Fang," corrects Jenny. "It's like something scored a fang down it. For such a clean site, there's a sloppiness right here. I have a small piece of saliva which is down the lab. But given the cleanliness of the rest of the site, I have no idea how they would get to the item."

"How big is the item?" asks Kyla.

"Four inches, according to the curator."

"So you could carry it in your mouth?"

"Yes," says Jenny, "but there really are no other signs of invasion. A human would need support, need something to stand on, to operate from, even if it was just the racks. But nothing has been disturbed."

"And was this box sat on top? It didn't need to be lifted?"

"Yes, Kyla, sat right on top."

I can see Kyla has a train of thought about to round the bend. There's an animation in her that's been missing and if you wait for it, she'll flick her hair with just a twist of her neck. A kind of smug, I got it, I have seen before. But the best bit is it exposes her neck. It was the hook that caught me and I'm still attached to the line.

"If I said someone flew a drone in here," says Kyla, and there goes the hair, yep that neck's still got me, "and then cut the box before grabbing the cup and flying out, you'd say what to me, Jenny?"

Jenny lifts her hand to her chin and I see the rebuttal coming.

"I'd say I haven't seen a device with a cutter and a grabber of a light enough construction, but even if one was available, and that is a distinct possibility given the mods that can be made on these things, drones don't drool."

"Exactly," says Kyla, "but animals do. Ones with wings."

Chapter 3

"Wings? Like a stunt bat?" It's not as daft as I make out, for I have seen things in these last months that make no sense at all but you need to challenge everything, otherwise we start to accept that the unicorns are coming to save us.

"Yes, I know," says Kyla, "It's a theory that works but it does mean the Darkness would be involved. Something of that ilk anyway."

"Jenny?"

"It is a workable theory, Trimble. We'll see what the DNA test throws up. I'd rather wait before I go along fully with the notion."

"Okay. Let's see if we can substantiate it then. I need that curator for a description of the cup."

"Well you go get him then, I'll get the coffee," suggests Kyla, "Jenny?"

"No, I'm good, but he's been without one for five minutes, so he'll be getting cranky."

"You okay, getting them?"

"Dammit Mulgrew, I'm in a wheelchair, I'm not useless. It's just coffee and I'll get one of those cardboard carriers. And if I need help I'll ask. It's just a damn wheelchair."

Kyla pushes herself off and I feel like I just mashed up the egg shell real good. I watch her disappear down the long racking and part of me wants to carry her, hold her and take her everywhere she wants to go. But she'd hate that.

"Don't take it to heart, she's frustrated, pissed at her legs, not you."

"No Jenny, she's pissed at me. I keep trying to do things for her."

"Yes okay, she's pissed at you. You always did try to control. Try to make it right too much. She's a strong willed, determined woman. Don't direct her, don't try and take all the problems away. We cope, Trimble."

"I know but…"

"Kyle! We cope. You screwed it up with me. Don't lose that one. She's too far into you for it not to hurt her plenty."

"Is it that obvious?"

"Yes," says Jenny and walks up to me and places a small kiss on my forehead. "For one who was right there, yes, it's bloody obvious."

"Sir, I mean, Trimble, this is Dr Martin Magoro, the curator of this particular section."

As I turn I am dwarfed by the one of the largest African men I have ever seen. He reaches out and takes my hand, which I fear for, before realising he has just the right sense of how strong a handshake should be.

"Dr Magoro, I'm Detective Trimble, this is forensic officer Tatler and you've met Officer Kobold. Thanks for your time, sir. I really just want to get a description of the item from you, especially the markings on the cup."

"The wooden chalice, it's more than just a cup," says the large man in a deep voice that could shake the racking around me into submission. "You see there's definitely a celebratory element to this chalice. I've never seen a match anywhere and within the era it's associated with in Haiti, I don't think I have seen anything similar."

"What do the symbols mean?" asks Jenny.

"I don't know, they are unlike anything I have ever seen within Haitian culture. In fact, if it hadn't been found with the other items I wouldn't even have said it was Haitian. The wood and chalice style is in keeping but the symbols are not."

"Would you be able to draw the symbols out for me? Just a sketch so I can check it with a few of my colleagues."

"By all means," replies the expert, "but in truth, this is not a great loss for the museum, I doubt it has even been displayed, such an anomaly as it is."

"Still, I'd like to know who has it and why? Kobold, get the good doctor a pencil and some paper so he can make the drawings."

I let Kobold take the curator away to complete his drawings and then turn to see Kyla return with the coffees.

"The invalid's back, oh and look, she's managed."

"Okay, thanks," I say, taking my coffee. "Sorry."

"How are things coming along?"

I update Kyla with what's happened and then sit to sip my coffee. I let Kyla and Jenny talk away about something or other but my mind's on the case. Unknown symbols and never been displayed. The hairs on my sleuthing neck are rising. After the turmoil of the bomb planting and the craziness of all the killings and possessions of people, things have just started to seem normal again. But something is saying not for long.

But I have a concert to get to with a woman who needs a night out. And I want to see that dress on her again. Yeah, I need to park this issue with someone who knows for a few hours while I give Kyla some time. I'll get the drawings and send them to Sister Martha, my blind nun who sees more than anyone. If there's anything strange about it, she'll know.

"Trimble, I have the drawings for you."

"Nice one, Kobold, not even a single sir in there. You're improving. Here's a number I want you to send the drawings to. Then get them scanned in at the station. If you need me, I have the phone. Otherwise, I'm off for some classical education." Kyla smiles. It's good to see.

About two hours later, I'm done up like a kipper in a tuxedo, returning to my flat having popped out for some last minute items while Kyla finished off getting ready. Opening my door I see the red dress that sits neatly on her motionless legs. Tracing the line up, I enjoy the curve of her hips, the expanse of flesh at her torso and then the gorgeous hair that frames a beaming face.

"It makes it worth it, seeing your face, Mulgrew."

"I'd take your jeans and T-shirt any day but Kyla, that is stunning."

"Shut up and push!"

I drop my minor purchases on the table and take up her new chariot. The fact she's letting me push is a concession as no one else would get the chance, she's too keen to show she's no invalid. Once in the taxi, we sit in the rear, quiet with just a single hand held. Sometimes you just have to appreciate the moment.

There's a vibration in my pocket. I ignore it. Then it starts again. I don't want to answer the mobile so I let it go again. And then there's a different vibration. That's a text. I'll just check that one. It's from Sister Martha. Just three words. Get here now.

"What is it?" asks Kyla. I show her. She looks at me eyes showing deep concern, pondering what it means. Then there's a simple nod and she turns to the driver.

"Err driver, change of plans..."

Chapter 4

We arrive at the Cathedral where Sister Martha lives and it takes a moment to build the wheelchair up again so that Kyla can wheel herself into the building. After previous engagements working with the now dead Father Krystanovic, the people at the cathedral know me well and apparently Sister Martha has told them I'm coming. Fingers point just as soon as we are recognised.

She's in her cell, sat on her bed with printouts of the drawings in her hand. Her wimple is pulled back and her face is gazing at the printouts, her face with no eyes. Despite this infirmity, the sister sees everything, as previous dealings with her remind me.

"We were awaiting his move and now it has happened. Now the Darkness will begin to build a terror, now it will unleash the rage and anger in people to destroy their enemies. There will be no love shown, no mercy to those in the way."

Good evening to you too. "I see you have the drawings. What is it that was taken, Sister? Is it a weapon? Something valuable."

"Sit, Trimble. And Kyla, you poor child, still no movement. I don't think she requires a doctor, Trimble, she requires cleansing. That is no medical condition."

I sit down on the nun's bed opposite her and Kyla wheels herself close. The poor sister is looking even worse than ever, her skin shrivelled on her hands. She took a battering trying to stop the Darkness arriving, one she is still recovering from. In truth I don't think any of us survived the first battle unscathed.

"The symbols speak of possession and control. It invokes a demon of the lower realm but don't let that fool you. This is a creature that feeds on hate and loathing. And one that will not hesitate to take a person to the point of doing incredible damage to those that they really love. It is single minded, spiteful and brutal. "

The nun seems to rest for a moment and I look across at Kyla who doesn't take her eyes off the nun. I wait respectfully but there's something bugging me.

"Sister," I say, "Why did they take the cup? What does it do? Summon the demon? Control it."

"No! It will not be controlled. Understand that Trimble. You cannot control this."

"Okay," I come back trying to calm the situation. She's clearly still touched by the defeat and the loss of the Father, her friend.

"Then what, Sister?" asks Kyla gently.

"Listen carefully. They will entice someone in pain, someone who has a grudge and they will say they can help them get justice. But it will be a bloody justice. And first they will ask for innocent blood. The person will collect innocent blood and drink it from the cup. Then will the demon enter them. But for its target, the person must be marked with something of the victim. Otherwise it will just randomly obliterate whatever it comes across."

"But who would follow that? Drink an innocent's blood. Kill an innocent." Kyla shakes her head.

"Be under no illusions," retorts the nun, "this is enacted by people of desperation, people of spite, who cannot forgive. And there are plenty in this city. But now go, you have your information." The sister lies down and I turn to Kyla who shrugs her shoulders to ask if that's it. I shoo her away with my hands.

As Kyla wheels herself out, I kneel close to the sister's head. "Are you okay Martha? You're always curt but not this cold."

"I'm sorry Detective but life is running low for me. The battle almost ended me as it did my friend. And now I struggle to sit up. I can't even get about like your friend. I am fading, Trimble, I doubt I will last long. It seems that my name is known and they are seeking me. And not with guns and bombs before you offer your protection. On a spiritual plane they attack, and there my body is sorely wounded."

"What can I do? I need your guidance."

"No you don't. Just stay humble, stay calm and seek out the best in people. And don't be afraid to shoot when you see someone to save. Now go and find this cup. From there you will find the murderer-to-be."

So I have to find a wooden cup in a city this size and in fact even before it's used I have to check if anyone is vengeful. I need to concentrate on the cup. Where to start? Who has seen it? Where would you go to find out about using it? I think I need to scour the underworld contacts, see who is offering death.

I walk outside the cathedral where Kyla is waiting in her chair. The air is cool and Kyla only has her perfect dress on.

"So Mulgrew, are we on a date or what?"

I walk round in front of Kyla and kneel down, drinking in the sight of the dress and her figure setting it off. Why now?

Why not tomorrow, preferably after midday. We need this night, we need this time. I feel her hand reach out and drag my head forward holding it tight to her chest as she runs her hands through my hair. I love it but I know what it means. This is the expulsion of a hunger, of a chance now disappearing. She moves my head away and kisses my head.

"Time to work, Mulgrew. But I ain't wearing this for no search. And you ain't no James Bond so that tux needs changing."

I pull out my mobile and call for a cab. Twenty minutes, and it's cold. I turn to Kyla and bend down, scooping her up off her wheelchair. I plonk myself onto it, gripping her tight on my lap and pull her in close. It begins again. I can feel it. That sense of dread, that sense of foreboding, I need to be ready. But for twenty minutes, I'm going to hold the best thing in my life close to me. Who knows how we'll look on the other side of this.

Chapter 5

I hand Gonzales some notes and ask him to put them up on the screen. After managing to save so many people from death during the arrival of the "Darkness", my reward has been to have my department expand permanently with Gonzales, Hughes and Kobold and to have access to the street guys whenever I want. This is good. We also have new rooms from which to work. This is bad. They have modern computers and screens and I am at a loss.

Kyla laughed heartily when she heard I had ordered and placed a revolving chalkboard in the main conference room. The others are probably laughing too but I'm the boss so you don't laugh too loud. And they certainly ain't laughing now, sat around the long table and wondering what the panic is? I'm not sure but...

"Okay guys, or team, or invested associates, whatever we are meant to say today, we have a problem. Kobold, run them through the theft."

I sit down and listen to my officer's take on the robbery. She doesn't mention a winged thief, but does point out the bizarreness of the method of extraction. There are also sketches of the chalice on the clever screens we now have and the drawings from the curator are also shown. When she's recounted everything she gives me a smart nod and sits down. I think she still thinks of herself as the junior and she is the least experienced. But I don't have juniors, we only have each other.

My notes are put on the screen by Gonzales and I run through the briefing from Sister Martha. Their faces are grim. Good. No one's believing this is just wild imaginings from a nun. But then Gonzales and Hughes were there when we got attacked by some evil chicken. There was the priest who nearly blew Gonzales and a congregation to hell. And Kobold saw the woman with the entrancing eyes and snakes emerging from her hands. I rub my injured hand, right over where I lost both fingers. They never found her body.

"Sir?" said Kobold.

Dammit, I was miles away. "It's Trimble, Kobold, always Trimble. Hughes, what do you think?"

The powerfully built woman, mother and best sergeant I know, looks thoughtful. "Well, it's only been about 24 hours so they may or may not have been using it already. If it needs innocent blood then we need to check through today's reports of homicides, see if we can trace a source through them. Also a mark of the victim? Need to know what that means. Today's thefts need going through. I recommend you base one of us here and get a small team of uniforms or civilians to go through everything that's happening."

"Good Hughes. Let's set this place up Gonzales. Computers and whatever is required. But don't remove my blackboard." There's a small chuckle. "Hughes get me some staff, tell the Chief I think it's something big and that it's "Darkness" related. He'll not bat an eyelid. While you do that, I'll take Kobold and see if any street sources have anything. And then I'll pick up

Detective Corstain. She might not be ready for active duty outside but she can sure handle this end."

I watch them get up and move off to their tasks before heading back to my office. No longer do I have a desk in a sea of desks but instead I am insulated in my own cupboard. The major benefit is that I managed to install a hammock. No more crashing in an empty cell. I'm not sure if Kyla would fit in there with me and I'm not that unprofessional. Mind you, I'd like to be.

As I gather my thoughts of who to go to on the street, the telephone lights up a button that says "Chief" and I don't answer, instead just hauling my ass up the two flights of stairs to his office. He took over during the horror of my previous Chief blowing his brains out and he has been totally straight with me. So straight, I trust him.

His office is stunning, nothing out of place, plaques, pictures on the wall, even a neat shredder and bin beside his desk. He's eating an apple as I enter, from a bowl of fruit on a side table. Even his diet's terrific.

"Trimble, Gonzales briefed me, you haven't got a lot."

"No Chief, but the nun was adamant, totally convinced. I've learnt to take a lead from her in these matters. Maybe we can get ahead this time. The body count was high last time."

"Not as high as it could have been. I hear you are bringing Corstain back to run the office. How is Kyla?"

"She's frustrated but she's capable. Better for her to be here than to sit around in the flat doing nothing."

"And they still don't know what's causing the paralysis?" asks the Chief.

"No, it's spiritual, at least that's what Sister Martha says."

"Okay, bring her back but keep an eye. She's been through a

lot. I know you're close but you're the senior officer and might have to call against her. If you can't, I'm here. But I agree, she'll be best used here."

I turn to go but he calls me back. "And Trimble, after the way this place was infiltrated last time, anything significant, anything they can use, doesn't leave your team. No significant briefings to me over the phone either. We'll meet outside, away from here, after all who's to say they haven't bugged here."

That's a point. No police mobiles. We'll need to use our own. It kind of feels good knowing the guy above me is looking at the wider angle. I'm not sure I can raise myself to see that view.

"So here Trimble, that's a mobile number only you have. Call me when there's anything significant I need to know or do. Coffee house is probably the best thing. You do like coffee?"

You'd think that would be highlighted on my service record.

Chapter 6

One of the joys of having been a beat cop before working my way up is the sheer number of rather shady people I am acquainted with. Some I have leaned on, some bought, some used and some just plain destroyed, in a criminal capacity of course. One of these people is Louis Colhorne, once a small time drug dealer before he got into the gang warfare. A nasty piece of work but also someone who knows a lot, especially about vendettas and takedowns.

He hangs out in a classy club downtown, somewhere that high quality drugs are available to very important people. But he started by pedalling the lower classes and he has a handle on everyone that talks below and how they are shut up. So he'll know the hits that will be made. I'm thinking that someone who wants revenge and who has the money will take out a hit on the innocent rather than do it themselves. Worth a punt.

Kobold is in simple jeans and jacket with mean black boots. This shouldn't be a problem, asking these sort of questions to Louis but I've made sure Kobold is packing enough for both of us. She pulls our unmarked car over in front of the club and a doorman comes over to move us on.

"This is a private club and that is a private space, so push it sister. Move on."

Man, he's greasy. Dressed up in a quality suit but he's no class act. However beyond him I can see four gentlemen who do look classy and extremely muscular. I'd love to just get out and punch this guy but the job won't get done.

"Hey, don't get all heavy on the girl. She might just snap back."

"And who the hell are you, grandpops? Out looking for a coffee morning."

That was the trigger. I can take all the usual insults until the cows come home but since I've been with Kyla, I'm kinda anxious about the age difference. And as for grandpops. The wee shit!

Reaching forward, I grab the doorman by his tie and pull him half into the vehicle. I grab his nose hard, twist and punch him, causing him to fall backwards on the pavement. The heavies are moving, so I step out of the car and flash a badge.

"Trimble! I want to talk to Louis. Got some advice about picking doormen."

The heavies are too experienced to react and one asks politely if the lady and I will accompany them inside and he'll see if Mr Colhorne is available. I smirk at the doorman and thank the heavy, agreeing to follow him. Kobold does a good job of looking calm as I take the lead.

We are shown to a small room with a comfortable sofa, drinks cabinet, and a large television. The heavy who showed us in, remains standing impassively by the door. For two minutes, we sit motionless, and I chew over my lines. Then the door bursts open.

"Well, well, Trimble, and a very fine lady. Pleased to meet you Detective..."

"This is Detective Kobold. And this is no social visit, Louis.

I need your help, a matter of some urgency."

Louis nearly chokes. "Me, you want my help. After all those narcotics busts you made on me. Unprovoked too."

I laugh. "We caught you on five occasions."

"Caught who? Some malcontents that had chosen to use my club. I was never even charged."

"Well this is more pressing than all that. I need to know if there's any unusual hits going down. Payment to take out someone that they have no beef with. Weird ones."

Louis is dressed in a dinner jacket and trousers and rubs his hands along the edges of the jacket. "What makes you think I'm into that sort of thing? I run a good business here, people know not to mess with me."

"But you'd know. A man in your position needs to know in case anyone is daft enough to try."

Louis nods and then turns to his heavy, waving him out of the room. He walks over to the drinks cabinet and asks if we want anything. It's too early, and I don't trust him to go order a decent coffee, so I decline.

"You did a good thing when you stopped those bombs, Trimble. I had a niece in the stadium. So I guess I owe you for that. But I warn you be careful chasing this lead. Hitmen don't like to be known. This one won't like it and he won't know I know of him. It stays that way."

"Of course."

"It came in the other day, from somewhere you don't want to ask about. The target seemed weird and very unusual. I also don't agree with targeting the clergy. I believe the buyer had said that the target didn't matter but just make sure it was clergy. And they wanted a sample of blood mailed to them. That didn't seem like a business decision to me."

"So who's the hitman?" asks Kobold.

"Hey lady, I have been polite, but I talk to the boss okay. He's done a good thing for my family but you don't get to speak." He almost spits the comment at Kobold.

"Louis, Kobold defused the bombs hanging on the edge of the dam. You probably owe her more than me." I smile politely.

Louis comes over to Kobold and takes her arm. "My apologies. You have my thanks. Karen is very dear to me."

"Accepted," says Kobold. "Who is it?"

"He's a hitman. You won't have been around too long, they don't advertise their name. But this one can be seen leaving his home. It's in a good district. And I think it's today, the hit. So you need to move. Just an address, Trimble. And it didn't come from me. And no pen and paper. Keep it in your head. Just a hunch, saw something passing by. Understood?"

"Perfectly, Louis."

"234, Cromberfield. Take care, he's good."

"Thanks, Louis."

"Sure Trimble, this is in return for Karen. Don't make it a habit."

I nod and get up to leave. But Louis steps before Kobold and takes her hands, kissing her on either cheek. "If you weren't a cop, I'd give you a reward. Don't ever come after me, I'd hate to have to put you down."

I wonder how Kobold will react. She's not used to these situations. Early twenties and getting the treatment from an old pro. But she does me proud.

"Don't worry," she says, "If I'm after you, you won't see me before I put you down."

Chapter 7

I get on the blower to Hughes and ask how things are coming along. Apparently Gonzales has got his room almost up and running and has sent a car for Kyla. Hughes has picked up a reported homicide and is enroute to see if it's anything to do with the chalice. She hasn't a lot more details but of the three deaths in the last 24 hours it seems the strongest possibility.

Kobold is driving and we get to an address in a suburban part of town that says families, softball and parades. There's not a lot of crime here so I guess it would be a heck of a hideout for a killer.

The street lights are on as it's dark, the light fading about seven these nights. We drive past the address only once and I get Kobold to park two blocks away. If this guy is good then we need to be careful. I'm also aware that I need this guy alive. That might be harder than not, I doubt he'd come quietly, and then will he talk? But it's a lead.

I decide we need to be very discreet and so I order Kobold to hop through some back yards and take up a surveillance position. Sitting in the car is murder as I can't see what's happening and I told Kobold to keep the communications to a minimum, texting when the target leaves. But it also means I get to stop and think. At the moment the whole approach is so scattered, looking for the needle in the haystack, unsure of where the terror will come from. Last time it was a flurry of murder and mayhem and I'm expecting no different. This is the calm before the storm.

Kyla calls. "We are live at NASA ground control, Mulgrew. Thanks for bringing me in, I wouldn't have been good at home."

Home. She called my flat home. I know it's where she's been sleeping but even so. Home has so many other connotations than lodgings or dwelling. Still, I doubt we're going to see it much this week.

"Keep me updated about Hughes. I have a lead but it may be only one thread, there could be plenty. This city's full of people who want to get their own back on others."

"Will do. And I saved the dress. You still owe me a posh night out."

"It's coming, I promise."

And she's gone and I get my mind back to Kobold, hiding in the bushes of a house. It starts to rain and I feel bad for her. Not bad enough to swap places but still, I've been there. And then it starts to pelt down. I'm thinking about taking a spin past the house when a text arrives. *He's moving.*

I can feel my heart begin to beat faster, the chase is on. But I wait for a second text. *Clear.* I spin the wheel and drive down the street parallel but down from the house we were watching. Kobold clears a hedge and gets in. She's sodden.

"Quick, Trimble. Up on the right." We drive past the man walking the street. He's about five foot nine and dressed in a raincoat, head covered by a large hat. He's got a bag, with carry handles like a small case for the aeroplane. I don't slow down and drive past, turning along a road where I pull in. Jumping out, I see Kobold slide over and take the wheel. Damn, it's still pissing down.

I move to the shadows and watch the man cross the street. Then I wait before moving up to the street corner. Without stepping into the street light, I see him cross the next street. Doubling back, I reach the parallel road and jump into the car which Kobold has brought back around.

"Straight ahead, two blocks."

She drives quickly and drops me. I run to the street corner, up from where I got out, and clock my target heading for the train station. It's a small stop and he calmly walks in. I telephone Kobold and ask her to tail the next train. No easy task but I can update her.

Entering the station, I can't see him. There's no large hat, no one with a bag, it's like he vanished. So I scan everyone. Every male but none fit his build. And then I see the woman waiting. She's a bit odd for a woman. The dress is not picking up any curves. I try to look away and not stare. The legs are strong, but the hips just seem too slim.

Scanning the rest of the station, I reckon no one else fits the bill. I retire to the restroom and take off my coat. Underneath I have a sports jacket on and I remove my large hat for a beanie. I take out my sunglasses and don them. It's not the best disguise but it might do. I dump my clothing in a locker and purchase a ticket into the city. Picking up a paper at the stand behind my target, I see the strangely built woman has a small bag. It could have been carried inside the holdall.

A train pulls up and I get the carriage behind the one she gets into. As I hold onto the rail, I text Kobold that I am on the departing train. But there's another message. Apparently Hughes has a hit. Blood taken from a victim. A victim with no record. Messaging that I am in pursuit, I ask her to chase that lead. The train pulls off and I juke my head to see into the carriage beyond. My target is sitting calmly, reading a smutty woman's novel with a man whose chest has been removed of all clothing adorning the front.

But I look beyond him. I see two nuns conversing. Shit, that could be it. And I'm in the carriage behind. I start to sweat. Surely he won't do it on the train if he wants to collect the blood. I pray not because at this time, I am helpless to prevent anything he does.

Chapter 8

I need to slow down, can't be too overeager as he'll see me and may either run, or worse, do the deed right now and take out more targets than he intended. *Ease back Kyle, ease back.* I send a text to Kobold, updating her, while my brain runs through where the nearest convents are, nearest churches, working out where these nuns are from. If it's a hit then this must be their normal route. So how did he know they would come this way, he would have had less than a day to prepare?

The train comes to a halt in a station and I hover by the door in case the nuns and my hitman leave. But the two sisters remain in conversation with each other and he doesn't come up from his paper. And the train moves off again. Next stop is Angel Island. It's a park with a statue of a saint at the far end. I text Kobold, asking if she knows anything about the place. Waiting for the reply, I sneak a good look at my man. I can't even tell if he's carrying. Maybe it's a knife. Maybe he'll tail them in the park and slash them.

The vibration in my pocket tells me Kobold's replied. A week of veneration at the shrine in the park. Of course, these sisters are random but there will be sisters going to this at all times. Dammit. The stop's approaching and I move to the doors upsetting a youth from listening to their music as I catch their leg. He goes to get up to complain but I can't get engaged. The jab is hidden from view but it's very potent and he falls back into his seat, quietly wheezing, the wind knocked out of him.

My hitman is on the move still disguised as a large woman. He almost ambles off the train and I wait until the doors are about to close again before jumping off. My heart's racing as we are getting to the point when he'll make his move. I see the sisters walk off towards the park, the battered iron gates permanently open and the corroded sign swinging in a light wind. The rain has stopped but the air is still cool.

The hitman is about ten feet behind the sisters, making a great show of struggling along. Not wanting to get seen if he casts a look around, I slip off the path into the trees, the damp moss making it hard going to stay in touch. It's not autumn thankfully and the leaves are still blowing above me. The paths in the park have lighting but it's discrete, highlighting colours here and there. Sticking to the shadows is easy enough but I'm aware this guy is a pro.

He turns his head and I slide behind a tree. I can feel the moment, this is the scan to make sure he's alone with them. I give it two seconds and then juke my head out. The large coat is dropping and he has a knife in his hand, big enough to be a machete. I draw my weapon. "Halt, police!"

He turns and I see his hand going to his pocket. I just fire. It's a gamble but he's a pro and he'll shoot better and faster. My bullet tags his arm spinning him round. But it's his non-firing arm and I see the small gun raise as he completes the spin. I move left, instinctively and the shot passes by me, too close not to disturb. But I fire again and catch his leg. He falls and his gun drops from his hand.

I run to the gun and kick it away before he can recover. The sisters are screaming. I stand beside the man, gun pointed at him. I toss my phone at the sisters. "911, tell them assistance required. Perpetrator apprehended. Detective Trimble requires assistance, now!"

The nuns stare at me but I insist on them making the call. Surely Kobold has heard the shouts. The hitman is moaning in pain. No doubt his mind is desperately trying to find a way out. My blood is racing around me, causing a pounding in my ears. There's a slight shake that I have to control, but they are safe. The nuns are safe.

There are footsteps running towards me and a flashlight bouncing along. "Police" comes the yell. It's Kobold.

"It's me, Kobold." The sisters are still holding my mobile but haven't done anything with it. "Call it in, I think the sisters are going to need help too, they're in shock." Kobold nods and picks up her mobile. And then I see him smile. My hitman just grins at me before biting down hard.

"No! Kobold, he's got something in his mouth." I dive down to him and prise open his jaws but there's foam coming from the mouth and he twitches a few times and then stops. I clear out the mouth and, making a tube with my hands, I breathe hard into him. And then I push down on his chest counting out.

It's another ten minutes before a paramedic pushes me aside. After they try for ten minutes, they call it. Kobold stares at me and then points to the sisters.

"I know Kobold, I know. But dammit, why did he have to kill himself? We needed a way in." There are blue lights everywhere now and I see uniform making a cordon. There will be statements before sleep tonight and questions about what happened.

But all my mind thinks is has Hughes gotten anything? It's coming and we need another lead because this one self-terminated.

Chapter 9

I get back to the station and receive a round of applause from the night crew. It's not how I feel but I smile to keep their morale up. No doubt they have their own problems tonight. Hughes meets me at the door and as soon as we get into the elevator she details the homicide she checked out. An old man, living alone, regular stalwart of the community, attacked and stabbed in the gut, blood everywhere. Definite possibility.

I ask if forensics have anything. She says not so far but Tattler's on the case. That's good. One thing that bothers me is that we have no way of knowing how quick this chalice can be used. Do they just grab blood, pour it in and go for it? And what's the mark they carry of their victim? There's too much that's unknown.

After stopping by to make a statement, I head for my task room and am blown away by the technology Gonzales has set up. Kyla's in her wheelchair and as the room's crowded, I merely touch her shoulder with my hand. She looks up and smiles. I smile back trying to let her know I'm okay.

"We're chasing everything from here. Every police call, we're tracking right across the city," says Kyla. "I had the Chief here to see it. He's upstairs still working on how many men he can shove our way. At least we're not alone this time."

I nod and point to my office. "Okay, go get some rest." In my office I pull my hammock across and, after setting my coffee machine up for two hours time, I lift myself up and roll into the swinging haven. Genuinely, I try to sleep but it won't come, just images of that man twisting when shot, and then his face, the grin as he killed himself. My brain says bring the nuns to mind, says you saved them but it's a darkness that occupies me.

The door opens and I hear Kyla curse as she hits the frame of the door with her wheelchair. Wheeling it over to my hammock, she reaches up and pulls herself into the now swinging piece of canvas and I grab her trying not to fall out in the process.

"Are you okay, Mulgrew?"

"No. He just killed himself right in front of me. Just like that, smiling, or at least grinning."

"It's starting again."

"Yeah, it is." I pull her close and share a moment. Part of me wants to get more intimate but I'm not sure a hammock is a great idea, especially in the middle of the station. One almighty collapse and the whole precinct will be taking the piss for the next year. So I hold her, tenderly, quietly, enjoying a moment's calm.

There's a yell in the air. Not far away either. I roll out of the hammock and then grab Kyla, lifting her down to her chair. Reaching for my gun before I exit the room, I hear another shout. Then a noise like someone has toppled a set of filing cabinets. I run out of the door and race towards the noise. The whole floor is up and looking for where it is happening. Then there's a flash of colour through the stairwell window.

I see Hughes across the way and nod at her to follow me. Pushing open the stairwell door, I see a uniform falling past me with a bloody face. There's no time to catch him and I move to where he came from. A man stands there, wild and bloodied. Without warning, he drills me with a foot and I tumble down. Hughes steps past and drives her shotgun butt into his face. He barely flinches.

She's caught with a smack across the jaw and I wonder how she's still standing as the man runs up the flight of stairs.

"Go, Hughes, go."

I follow her figure bounding up the stairs and see the swinging door where the man exited. Stepping through that door, I see him charging towards the Chief's office. The Chief steps out and is grabbed by the man, a large hand around his throat, squeezing. I drop to one knee and fire. It's an instinctive shot and a good one as I see the blood spurt from the head and the man falls.

"You okay, Chief?"

"What? Yes... yes I'm good. Who..."

The Chief is stunned into silence as the man gets back up to his feet, his head still bleeding. A hand grabs the Chief once again and I hear him choke. I fire my gun, hitting the shoulder and then the head again. But this time he doesn't flinch and keeps Chief in a choke hold. It's a strong hold as I see the blue coming into the Chief's face.

Running up to the man, I put my gun to his head and get covered by blood and other stuff as the top of his head explodes. But as I force myself to look, he's still squeezing. The Chief is expiring and this man, this thing has a grip we can't break. I grab his arm but the man throws me away with his other hand. And then Hughes is there, shotgun on his wrist. Blood splatters as it becomes detached by the point blank shot. As the man flails wildly, she calmly places the gun on his neck.

The floor is a mess with blood and other body bits. The Chief is on the floor with first aiders now running to him. I'm lying on the floor nursing a sore back from the throw, looking up at the face of a giant. Hughes stands grimly looking down at the man's remains, almost without passion.

And then her shoulders shake, a uniform takes the shotgun as it falls from her hand, and she falls to her knees, hands across her face. Dear God, what on earth was that? Where does a man push off bullets to the head? What the hell does this chalice do to a man?

Chapter 10

The city looks great from the roof, the lights holding a glow on the night sky that makes you think we are an alien hub, a beacon on some far away planet. That's the thing with my city, it's out on its own, the mountains shielding us from any other light from a nearby conurbation. And up here, the noise is subdued, never gone, but subdued. Only those blasted pigeons disturb you but right now they are sleeping.

Hughes is taking in some air. After the attack, she was taken by Kyla and a few others to the changing area and had a shower. Thirty minutes, she was in there, according to Kyla. Quiet the whole time too. Now changed, she's up here and I thought I should make sure she's good.

"Things don't get any easier these days, Hughes. But you saved the Chief's life."

Leaning on an air conditioning unit, she turns to me, her eyes wide and slightly out of control. "What was that, Trimble? People don't keep going that long. Shot through the head, not once but twice. That's a kill in any book, but that bastard just kept going. I've seen plenty but that was crazy, crazy stupid. Without the shotgun..., do we need to carry a sword, like a vampire hunter now? I used to deal with the drug dealers, and they were mean, they did things to their enemies that was sick. But this, this is unholy. Plain wrong."

I put a hand to her shoulder. "Yeah, it is. But it's not over, maybe barely begun. And the city needs you and me, so if you can't believe or understand, that's okay, but we need to deal with it before the city's ripped apart."

There's a nod of recognition and I look into her eyes. The hope's still there. She'll be good. Asking her to pop back down to the office in twenty minutes, I depart the roof and route to the station's main conference room to see the Chief. Forensics are still working on the scene so his office is out of bounds.

The room has an enormous table with smaller rectangular ones holding papers and coffee at the side. The Chief is at the far end, sitting down over reports.

"Trimble, how's Hughes? She really came up with the goods. That was way too close."

His fortitude is impressive but there's severe bruising on his neck, a deep purple that looks like a wild ink blotch. But he's in good spirits, a large steaming coffee on the table. There's not even a shake in his hands.

"She'll be okay. Who was it anyway? Did you recognise them?"

"Yes. One of the Langston brothers. I put them away twenty years ago, drug dealers and they blamed me for it all. And they should because I nailed those bastards when no one could touch them. They were always angry but that was the hothead, Joe. But he was never a man of great strength. That was like his rage, his anger, which was always off the charts, had been transferred to his muscles."

I take a seat beside the Chief, and he stops going through his papers. "We've got Kyla going through the reports and sending out forensics, trying to get a lead in. I'll see where this guy has been the last twenty-four hours. But unless we source this chalice, all we are going to do is clean up after the fact. I'll get back out and shake some feathers. Langston was old school, yes?"

The Chief nods profusely. "Yes, he had only been released a year and was keeping clean as far as we knew. You'd need to try some of the stars from back then to see what he's been up to. But he was being a good boy, I heard. And then this."

I nod and take my leave. Wearing the spare clothes from the office, I almost feel new despite the lack of sleep and the fact it's now four a.m. The centre hub we have set up is still busy, and I have a quick word with Kyla, who is showing a very concerned face. She's missing being out alongside me but she can't operate to a safe degree in her current condition. Not with these crazies on the go.

Grabbing Gonzales, and making sure we have some uniforms as back up, I head off to the salubrious district Langston resided in. The houses here are large, stunning and have a pool in the same way that most flats come with a toilet. There's not many lights on and as we approach Joe Langston's abode, I see his security gates have been compromised.

Technically I'm seeing a break in, so I get Gonzales to park up and enter the grounds of the house on foot, searching for a perpetrator. All is dark as I trace the wall to the side of the house. I wave at the uniforms to hold a perimeter and I make a run towards the front door.

It's been forced open and I can see no lights on the inside. Carefully I squeeze in and walk slowly along the hallway. It's a grand affair, delicate lights overhead that even look splendid when dark. There are pictures on the wall, some with celebrities of a bygone day. And then I hear something.

Someone is shuffling about in the room ahead. Easing myself to the door, I show Gonzales I have someone with a hand motion. Carefully, I try to peer in without disturbing the door to the room. But I can hear a liquid being sloshed about. And then I see it. The darkness gives everything strange depth and it takes a moment for me to grasp that I am seeing a pair of legs suspended in mid-air. And now there's a whoosh, followed by a burning smell. The room becomes alight with colour as flames ignite.

I kick open the door and see a hooded figure dropping a jerry can to the floor. "Halt, Police!" A knife is thrown and I dive to one side avoiding it. Gonzales comes through behind me and is tagged with another knife on the shoulder. The intruder runs to the back window of the room that looks out to the obligatory pool and simply crashes through it.

I get a shot off but it's wide and I run after the figure. The poolside is wet and the figure slips badly, its cloak now sliding away and revealing a milky white leg. The cowl also falls back and reveals red straggled hair, which looks strangely familiar. The slip gives me time to catch up and I fling myself onto the intruder as she tries to get up.

I've got a foot which makes her turn over and she tries to kick me with her other foot. As she sits upright, I see a revealing costume, striking and almost classy in its leather, but revealing nonetheless. The body is taut and the hair encircles a face I recognise. I battled her on the sand and then she threw snakes at me atop the city dam. Her body fell down from that great height but we never found the remains. But now she's looking right at me. And the eyes are ablaze with a wildness that scares me to the core.

Chapter 11

A kick connects with my head and I let go of her silky leg. Rolling onto my back, I feel her drive a knee into my groin and keep it there as she leans over me. Without those eyes, the view would be erotic, but the ungodliness, the sheer evil takes my breath away more than her clothing ever could.

"How's the bitch, Trimble? I hear she doesn't come running anymore. If bed time's no fun now, you know you can always have me." She lets go a wild cackle and I see my chance. I lift my torso up as much as possible and swing a fist into her side. It's not that strong but it unsettles her position and I am able to roll, causing her to tumble.

I round to my feet but she's already running to the garage at the side of the property. Tearing through the door like it's plywood, I can hear her inside kicking a motorbike into life. As I reach the door, I see her streak forward on the bike, breaking apart the garage door. Uniform are running up the drive but she's away past them before they even draw.

I run hard to the car, yelling at the uniforms to get Gonzales who's inside, and to call the fire department. Normally, I don't sit behind the wheel but no one calls my Kyla a bitch. Inside I'm a cauldron, raging at this woman who took my fingers and who has paralysed my girl. The car roars as I desperately look for her. There's no sign so I race ahead.

When my brain catches up, I put out a call for all units to see if anyone has eyes on. They'll not miss her if they see her. She's like some sort of glamour magazine advert, tons of flesh on a bike. Enticing but deadly. As I pass by a side street, I see the bike and a hooded figure on it. There's a pale white leg sticking out with a black boot on the end.

Swinging the car around, I try to intercept but she turns back and presents a smiling face, a grin of wicked intent. She's goading me. There's a distinct feeling that this is a trap. She waited for me but I can't help but follow. But I do call it in, requesting assistance.

We race through back streets, hurtling along but she takes winding routes doubling back and never giving me time to organise a roadblock. Then she makes a bid for the outskirts of the city, taking the route out of town to the wildlife park. The car is screaming at me as I push it to the maximum, and I wonder how crazy this pursuit would be during daylight, with a road full of traffic.

There's a call from despatch that a roadblock has been set up, maybe a mile ahead. I acknowledge and estimate us being there in thirty seconds but then she changes direction. A small dirt road, no more than a service road, not meant to be used by main traffic, sits at the side and she wheels around onto it. Following, the car bounces along and I feel like I'm on a fishing boat on the high seas.

I can see the edge of the wildlife park and she drops the bike and starts to make for its perimeter. Abandoning the car, I drive my feet forward in pursuit but she's easily more nimble than me. So caught up in this chase, I've even forgotten to call in my change of direction. She reaches the perimeter fencing of the park and I see a hole that she ducks through.

The ground is open, with some large rocks, sized like the creatures who inhabit this pen. As I struggle up a small hill, I hear the whimpering of an animal. As the moonlight shines down on a clump of bushes to my left, my eyes catch wolves, all lying close together, calling out as if in pain. It's like I'm listening to a chastened dog, not proud predators.

Normally I would fear the wolves but I swear they are more scared than me. Coming to the top of the hill, my brain is starting to yell trap. I'm in open ground, in an animal's pen and there's only one way out behind me. I reach the crest and realise my mistake.

Before me are a number of people in monk's habits. I've seen this before, and they were trying to sacrifice children then. Scanning around, I count at least twenty, and there are maybe more. I grab my mobile and hit the quick dial for the station. As it connects, I say "Trimble, Wildlife Park..." and then hear the line go dead. Looking up, I see what I surmise to be the block on my communications.

I've never seen a demon. There was an envoy but it was invisible. And how I wish this thing before me was invisible. It's got a head that resembles a goat but has longer horns, curved and proud like a stag, the face is a mesh between animal and man but where a goat would have thick curd eating gums, this mouth has the teeth of an alligator, pointed and designed to rip flesh.

The naked torso is that of a man, and a bloody strong one too, before the chest sinks into hips and hind legs of a hooved creature, fur or hair on the legs, so that all the skin is covered. There's no clothing and its genitals are fully on display. And kneeling before this monster is the woman I have been pursuing.

I feel the circle of monks around me closing in slowly. They are some distance away but their progress is ominous. I reach for my weapon, praying that backup can get here. The demon now places a hand under the woman's chin and lifts her to her feet. Her clothing is ripped from her and they are in a gross embrace, hands and features in places that should be kept private. It's grotesque and also intoxicating, perversely holding my horrified attention.

"What do you want?" I manage to blurt out.

Without breaking away from the demon and continuing her vile fornication, she snarls at me. "The innocent shall not speak. Bring forth the chalice."

A monk steps forward holding a simple cup. But it has markings on the side although at this distance I can't read them fully. But I can guess what they are. And I know whose blood they want to fill the chalice with.

Chapter 12

There's something engrossing about the strange scene, something that makes your eyes simply focus on the movement between this demon and its subject. As the circle of monks grows closer to me, I can't take my gaze from the naked woman, cavorting in an evil way with this thing before me. An urgency in me, created by the threat now posed is screaming inside my head for me to react but my horrified frozen stare continues.

The monks reach me and my arms are held. I am brought forward and my head covered with a sack. This causes such a kick of fear that I snap back to my primal instincts and kick out hard. The monk beside me grunts and I hear them fall to the ground. I get punched in the back and then thrown to the ground. Kicks and punches are now reigning down on me and pain comes from all angles.

I can barely move when the beating stops. It's been brutal but amateurish. If the drug dealers had administered this beating I wouldn't be able to think, nor walk or even move. But although I am in pain, I feel like everything still works. That being said, I shudder as they pick me up and then toss me onto a slab of some sort. My head is pinned down and the sack removed. Above me are hooded cowls and I can see into a few of them.

It's like they are entranced, totally devoid of emotion towards my plight, neither delighting nor grieving my predicament, and that is scarier than anything I have ever seen. There's nothing to appeal to and nothing to wind up. I have nowhere to go with this scenario.

And then a wild face of red hair and milky white skin appears over me. It takes its red lips and begins to kiss me on the lips. A hand roams my torso and I can do little but simply accept this intrusion. The figure breaks off and I see the eyes of hate looking at me, sizing me up like a toy, wondering whether to play with me or not.

"I wonder what it is she sees in you. A decent man, a hero, Sir Galahad running to her rescue. Still by her side though she's useless to you now, now that she can't perform. And I wonder why she can't perform. Just so you know before I drain your blood, just so you know, it was me. I crippled the bitch."

The woman laughs and then shouts at another monk. Looking straight up, I see a hand passing a doll, and a curved needle. The red head takes the items and then climbs onto the slab I'm lying on and sits astride me, wholly provocatively.

"Like this Detective Trimble? Been wanting this." Like any man, I would not shrink from a scene like this with the woman of my dreams. But this is a horror, bare as she is, a beast, a wild, embodiment of evil that taunts me and I take a solace that if she wanted to stimulate sexually she has failed. In fact I may even see disappointment there.

With a flash of annoyance, she holds the doll in front of my face. It's Kyla, and not just a simple representation. The face of the doll looks like Kyla's own face has been lifted and placed there. It is so lifelike. The rest of the doll is soft, like a kid's toy, but the face is like it's alive.

"When you thwarted me I made sure you paid. I drove this little tool into her spine, took away her legs. I made sure you couldn't have her the way you wanted. Broke apart your perfect little bitch."

I laugh at her. Laid at her mercy, I actually laugh at her. "You're jealous! You're actually jealous. This whole moment is because you are jealous of her." There's a break in the wild face, a panic. "You think every man would want you and before all others. And when they don't you become jealous. Look at you. This straddling me, being bare before me, all to show you can have me, tempt me and control me.

"I could have you right now," she counters.

"Maybe, but not willingly, not with enjoyment. Not with hunger. Merely flesh reacting to stimulus. Nothing other than that. You actually need me." As I laugh, she throws a punch at my head and it's a cracker, twisting my chin to the side. As I bring my face back to her, she holds up the doll, Kyla's face looking at me, and she drives the needle into her shoulder, slowly and deliberately. Then she wildly stabs the doll over and over again. And the face on the doll screams, it wails with Kyla's voice.

"That's the end of your bitch, Trimble. But it won't matter to you, because you'll be joining her in hell shortly. And your blood will fuel revenge on your colleagues at the police department. The last attack must have been a bloody mess. Your blood will create an even bigger scene. And in less than a day, we'll have enough blood to fuel a mass frenzy. There's nothing as potent as young, innocent blood."

She slides off me and places the screaming doll on my chest. "Best to die with your woman's voice in your head." There's laughter as she walks away, and then a simple instruction. "Slit his throat. Use the inductee."

There's a general dispersal happening and a reordering of monks. The sound of many footsteps retreating is a relief to me but a new circle of monks is forming around the slab. Kyla's voice is still screaming from the doll and I struggle to think past its sound. My body is held down by at least eight monks and the cowl leans forward right over my face. A strong arm holds a large knife above me, and I see my fate. But then a slender arm reaches out, shaking, and takes the blade.

"Drive it into his neck, and then gut him, right down the middle."

The slender arm shakes but the cowl that accompanies it nods before leaning in closer. I can see into the cowl now and there's a pair of scared eyes, eyes that belong to a young girl, maybe at the end of her schooling. There are glasses and make up applied badly, over used. And there's fear in her eyes. She's not much more than a child.

"Do it! Make your father proud."

The hand shakes, it waves back and forth. And then it raises up. The noise of a shotgun breaks the moment.

Chapter 13

"Cops, run!"

The knife falls from the hand above me and cuts into my shoulder but it's not that deep. My legs are freed as monks flee the scene. Instinctively, I roll over and grab the habit of the monk who was holding the knife. I hear another shot... and another. There's a cry of pain.

I fall over the habit of the monk I grabbed and make a desperate clutch for their leg. Grimly I hold on, hearing a voice telling the kid to run. The young voice protests that she can't and I hear the older voice say "Well then, goodbye."

I roll and pull at the leg hard causing the kid to fall just as a gun retorts from close range. There's a wetness hitting the back of my neck and the kid falls to the ground. With my other hand I pull the knife from my shoulder and roll back to face the older voice. But whoever owned it is gone. There's a whimper from the kid beside me and I rise up on my knees, checking the young one for injuries.

There's a serious neck wound, running deep and I can hear the air coming through the side of the neck. I take out a handkerchief and slap it over the wound, pressing down hard.

"Trimble? Trimble?" It's Hughes.

"Over here, need a medic. Get a damn medic, Hughes."

I lie there unsure of how long passes, holding on to the neck of the young monk. Some would say I was preserving our best lead but this is a young one and I really don't care what she's done. When the medics arrive, I roll clear and get to my feet, looking for Hughes. She's at a central squad car with a map, directing the search no doubt.

"Hughes, search in twos, threes if you can, no solo efforts. There's something with her. It's the woman, the body we never found. And there was a..." How do you describe that thing? "There was a demon with her."

"Okay, okay. I got it Trimble, go get a coffee, get straight, you look a mess."

I nod and head to the multitude of squad cars at the entrance to the wildlife park. As I walk along, I see the wolves hiding in the shadows, not looking for prey but actually hiding. On reaching a squad car, I grab a young lad and tell him to get a message to Hughes about the wolves, we'll need some of the park keepers to look after them. He nods and I see Gonzales.

"Hey, nice to see you. You haven't even brought donuts."

"You took off. You left me with a fire. Just be thankful you have a tracker on the car."

"Yeah, I know but it was her. And she's making it personal Gonzales, making it personal. Anyway, I need your mobile, think mine's in the car. Need to call Kyla."

I ring the precinct to get patched through and get Lewanski. There's a sorrow in her voice.

"Glad you're alive, Trimble, but I can't patch you to Corstain. She collapsed, crying out in pain, like she was being stabbed. She's in the back of a wagon, heading to the general hospital."

I drop the line. "Car! Gonzales, get in the damn car and drive, Kyla's gone down. Collapsed. Get the car ready I'll be back in a minute."

I leave him stunned and race back to Hughes. "Is there a doll, a kid's doll around?"

"Yeah," said Hughes, "bloody freaky, Corstain's face."

"Where? Where is it?"

"Evidence bag, think it's Joheim that has it."

I turn and scan the uniforms. He's quite a strapping guy and I spot him quickly. And he's holding the bag. "Hughes ring Sister Martha, tell her the general hospital. Detective Corstain brought in. Tell her to meet me and fast. Tell her to make it bloody fast."

Hughes probably replies but I don't hear as I run past Joheim and grab the evidence bag off him. There's a cry but I see Gonzales with the car turned and ready. Jumping in, we set off at a pace. There's no conversation, I need Gonzales going full guns on this one.

The drive is a blur. Images flash through my head, the demon, and the crazy animal human conglomeration that it was. The way it was cavorting with the woman, the way she had jumped on top of me, trying to stir me, like she wanted to take me from Kyla. And then the rebuke as she took Kyla from me. And the kid in the habit. What was that about? It was a teenager.

We race into emergency and a nurse comes for me on seeing my bloody complexion but I ask her for Kyla. She points to a side room, and I push open the doors marked "Strictly medical staff only." There's a number of beds but only one occupied and it has a doctor and two nurses attending. But there's also a nun in her habit.

"Sister. It was done with this." I hand her the evidence bag as she turns her eyeless face towards me. Taking it, she merely nods and I move round the bed to Kyla. She's got on a top that's covered in blood. Here and there it's been ripped and compresses have been applied. But she's cold. Very cold to touch. And she's not breathing.

"Time for a bit of trust, Trimble," says Sister Martha, "Time to make petition."

I lay my head on Kyla and I pray hard. Dear God, don't, don't take her. We need her, I need her. My ear touches her torso and I hear no breathing, no heartbeat.

"Sister, she's dead," says the doctor.

"No," says the Sister, in an almost dismissive tone, "only sleeping."

She's thunderous in her request to her God. She petitions Him based on everything He's ever done for people, naming countless occasions. And then I hear the doll ripping. She cries out again. Even harder. And there's a beat, a heartbeat. A slow rhythm now lifting in pace. A warmth starts to return to Kyla. I hear the doctor swear and the Sister slaps him round the back of the head.

"I'm done Trimble. Come see me in the cafeteria when you have spent a moment with her. I need to know what's happening. This doll shows me something else, something I need to pursue."

"Thank you," I say, almost in tears.

"It wasn't me. Upstairs, cafe, twenty minutes. If she wants to come up, bring her, but she might want a shower first."

Chapter 14

The hospital cafeteria is perfectly functional but, in honesty, doesn't have great coffee. I feel bad saying this as they do a different function really, feeding the numerous ill folk and medical staff that work here and coffee isn't their number one concern. Even so, I think it's something that needs attention.

I'm drinking my rather bland latte whilst opposite me, the strangest nun I have ever met sits quietly, almost brooding on something. I've known her a little while now and it's better to just give her the space rather than try to pry into whatever she's got on her mind. There was a time when I would have just blurted out something, anything to break a silence. But now, silence is actually a comfort.

"Get me some water, please."

And the silence is broken. Making my way to the serving counter, I ask for water and am promptly pointed to a table and dispenser across the room. There's a weariness in me as I reach the tumblers and pour my friend her drink. As I hold it in front of her face I think how bizarre it must look as this woman with no eyes doesn't flinch and I hold the glass in front of her face. A man a few tables away looks at me like I'm an idiot, and I can't really blame him.

"Just leave it on the table, Detective."

I set the glass down and sit down again. She takes the water and drinks it slowly as if it's something new to the palette. There's a small cough after she sets the tumbler down and I understand she's about to start.

"Have you given thought to the endgame in all this?"

"Honestly Sister, I haven't had time to think it through. Been crazy enough just getting after what few leads we had."

"Make no mistake, there will be an endgame, a reason for this mayhem. Last time it was a welcome but the demon is here now. I believe you saw it, at least its physical manifestation. So now it will want to make a hell in this city."

I cough. "Well, it's started. Trust me, Hughes having to blow the neck off an attacker who got back up after a bullet in the head was as close to hell as I have seen."

"I appreciate the scene must have been awful, Detective, but understand what bringing a hell will look like. This won't be a simple stirring of the ranks. It'll want to establish a kingdom, a place where bedlam rules. A place against everything good our city laws stand up for, and ultimately against everything my God is."

"You make it sound like a war rather than a series of abuses and murders."

Sister Martha lifts her head and points it at me. If she had eyes they would be transfixed on my face. "It's a war, Trimble. It was never anything else. The city is just the board we are playing on. Regardless, we know it has a following, you have observed followers, these unholy monks. And you have seen her, its queen. Be careful of her, for she will see you as a lead, as a general and she will try to turn you over."

I shiver remembering the red head sitting on top of me,

showing everything, trying to cause a sexual reaction. "She has tried. It's like a brutal assault of what should be a woman's subtle talents. But it's base, very base. It didn't work." There's some pride in those words.

"Careful, Detective. She'll come again but in more subtle ways. I am glad Kyla is restored to us. I would focus on her when this woman tempts, for she will. But beyond you and her, we need to think on what the endgame is. Imagine if the demon actually gained a foothold in the city, and then it could reach out to conquer the rest of it and more."

I'm struggling to understand where she's going with this doom-fest and I fail in not showing my annoyance, scratching my arm rather ambivalently. My face must be the opposite of wonder.

"I understand your reticence to think about conquest but this is why it's here. You saw the attack on the police chief. Imagine if you will, hundreds of people like that. All angry enough to follow this path of destruction, all prepared to kill an innocent to avenge what's been done to them. Look for the evil you can't stop. It'll send something you can't stop and then turn their passion for justice to vengeance and from there, the people will be controlled and set loose as an army."

I stand up and walk over to the table with the water, pouring myself a glass and then drinking it down. On my return to where we have been sitting, I am aware of the Sister being in prayer, head bowed.

"Take heart Detective," says the Sister rising, "we have the chance to stop it. It's time to fight, to scrap. It hasn't fallen onto your shoulders for no reason. There was a choice to make it you in the middle of this."

"So where do I start? And how long have I got?"

"I don't know Trimble but I can recognise you are exhausted. Go see her briefly and then go home and sleep before you go back into the office. There will be many upturned nights ahead. Go home, you may find some solace."

Popping downstairs to the ER, I see that they have moved Kyla. When I get to her ward, I see her flanked by uniforms but she is asleep. Touching her face and tracing her hair, I wish I could just climb in beside her. But I take the nun's advice and head home. Besides the nurse in charge of Kyla's ward looked pretty tough. I'm sure she'd be pretty angry if I just got in beside her patient.

Daylight streams through the windows and I close my blinds before stripping off and landing in my bed. I'm quickly out for the count. There's a nightmare, with a redhead cavorting with something wrong, just wrong. I can't even describe it but my mind knows it's wrong. There are more killings and faces of dead people. And then I see a knife dripping at me, feel my throat being cut and...

I wake in a sweat and shiver. But something tells me someone is in the room. I feel the covers thrown off me and someone lies on the bed, rolling me back towards them slightly. Reaching over to my gun on the side table, I feel a hand touch my shoulder. I'm all on edge and wondering how to confront this person when they remove the hand and pull the covers back over me.

"Mulgrew, just ease down. Don't turn round, just relax."

It's Kyla and I let her arms enfold me. There's a gentle kiss on my neck and I feel her bare skin pull close to mine. Lying there, I let her trace my body. And then she's just holding me before her hands go limp. The gentle snoring lets me know she's asleep. With one hand, I reach back pulling her even closer. Damn, this is good.

Chapter 15

The ring of the mobile wakes me suddenly and I spin over to get it from the side table behind me. I have to reach over Kyla to grab the phone and end up lying right on top of her. She moans lightly and smiles. Looking at the lighted screen the word "Kobold" sits in the middle.

"Trimble."

"You need to get down here. We have a situation with some of these strong freaks. There's a couple of children trapped in a school and we have several pumped up guys roaming the school, taking out whoever enters."

"Like the one at the station?"

"Yes, Trimble, exactly but they seem to be even rougher, more capable. We got a few headshots with the camera and are trying to get them identified but the Chief's asking for you. Says you might have an angle."

I tense up at this news and I feel Kyla's hands grip me, knowing something is wrong. "Okay, Kobold, on my way. Text me the location." Hanging up, I roll off Kyla and throw back the covers allowing myself to get up.

"Mulgrew, what's up?"

"Kids trapped with these bloody madmen on the go." I say this while my eyes take in a full view of Kyla on the bed with the covers lying clean off her. "And you have legs? Dammit girl, you have legs." I bend forward and kiss her hard but very briefly. "So use them and let's go."

She's dressed before me and grabbing the car keys. As I pull my pants up, I watch her holster her weapon, and it hits me what we are walking into. It should be a time of celebration, a time to do all the things her body couldn't do with the paralysis but instead she's going into the danger zone again. There's never time.

"I'll bring the car out front, Mulgrew. Whereabouts are we going?"

I check my mobile again. "Carbuston. Happy Valley Middle school."

"Doesn't sound that happy to me," she says racing out the door. It's a dull joke but in the tense moments sometimes you just have to say them.

The blue lights above the car beam out as Kyla weaves through the traffic. Even if we didn't have the address, we could have found the place from the helicopters circling overhead. News hounds, never missing a beat. After flashing a badge to the patrolman on duty, we get through to the inner cordon. The Chief calls me over.

"There are at least three of them, and you may have trouble as two are some sort of mercenaries. I have the SWAT team ready to go in but they are requesting you join them to help with tactical. I have said no, that we'll wire you up instead and you can sit in the control room, helping with liaison watching the screens. There are also at least ten kids in there scattered about. So far we've been able to tag these guys down, firing shots through the windows but who knows where the kids are hidden. It's a damn mess."

"Okay," I reply, "truck?"

"Over there."

"Did they read the report from the one at the station?"

"Yes, Trimble, they have had those reports."

"Good." I turn away and Kyla follows me. I hear the Chief shout after her, "Nice legs." Another mood breaker. He's extremely worried.

I show a badge at the truck and announce myself. A woman in a blue SWAT outfit grabs my hand. "Savage. The boss is inside."

I climb up the steps and enter what could be a TV production wagon. Along one side is a heap of screens showing a squad of heavily suited people with weapons, from different points of view.

"Trimble, I'm Farra, squad leader. Sit down, we're in position. Let me run this but if you see anything or have any important info, just say it. The live mic is in front of me. Press the switch when you want to transmit. We'll hear all of the team."

I nod and sit down, my heart racing and I try to focus. Kyla's outside due to the confines of the truck and part of me is glad we haven't been required to race into the action. I spotted Hughes and Kobold milling about when I made for the truck and no doubt they will have briefed the necessary people anyway.

"Move out, all teams move out to opening points."

It's like a video game watching from the camera on someone's shoulder. You could almost grab a joystick or a mouse and start directing them. There's still good daylight and the images are clear. I watch the teams begin their sweep of the building. Within a minute, they have seen a child. The heartbeat rises as one of the squad calls to her and she tentatively steps towards the screen. A pair of hands is seen grabbing her and two of the team break off to escort her to the world outside.

"Nine to go," I say under my breath.

"At least nine, we don't have exact numbers, Trimble. We need to search the whole area."

I nod. Then there's a flash of something up ahead on one of the cameras. Someone had crossed up ahead. The team seem to snake up the corridor. The something comes back and starts down the corridor towards them. There's two quick shots and the figure flips backwards to the floor. The cameras approach carefully but quickly.

"Tango down," says one of the team. Just then the other team have a target. Again two quick shots. "Tango down."

I see the cameras lift off their targets, moving on past them. "No!" I yell. "Take the head off, they need to take the head off. Hughes had to blow the bloody head off."

Farra relays the message on the communications but I see cameras fall forward, others running. There are cries of pain, and sounds of bodies being ripped. "Reform and assess," shouts Farra but the cameras are everywhere. And then there are kids in the cameras, lots of them, maybe six or seven. I see one of the madmen heading their way.

I spin on my seat and call for Kyla and Hughes. Farra is running up behind me too, weapon drawn. The Chief shouts over but there's no time. I run into the building through some double doors.

"Noise, make noise, we have to entice them away from the kids." I hurdle up some steps and go through double doors into a gym hall. Hearing screaming, high pitched, I race to the far end and go through more doors. There's a child in the hallway and I see her pointing up ahead. On reaching her, I can see a large man with a child held by the neck, and the child is turning blue. He's cursing the kid, screaming at it. But he's also referring to it as "my child".

I drop to a knee and draw my weapon. Kyla's over me and drawing hers too. We fire and the bullets hit the man but his grip doesn't fail. The child continues to choke. I start to run but Kyla's ahead of me. We need to release that grip.

Chapter 16

Kyla jumps the man who still has the child in a grip. Despite her leaping at him, the man is able to stay upright, Kyla hanging onto him. I dip my shoulder and hit him with everything I have. There's a moment when I feel I'm about to just bounce off but he eventually starts to tip and then falls to the ground. His hand still holds the child. As I roll away from the mess on the floor, I hear Farra shout get clear and then there's a gunshot.

As I rise to my feet I'm expecting to see blood and gore but instead the man is missing a hand and Kyla's got the child in her arms, throwing away a bloody appendage to the wall. There's no screaming from the child but Farra is standing over the writhing figure of the man who is shouting in agony. Hughes steps forward from behind Farra and bludgeons the man's head with her shotgun butt three times. And he's gone quiet.

"Kyla, get the child out, Gonzales, go with her for cover."

She nods and I don't have time to watch her depart with a child in complete shock but no longer blue in the face. Looking across to Farra, I simply get a nod, indicating that we move further down the hallway. Farra takes the lead and we round the bend at the end of the hallway. There's movement and a man's raging voice from ahead. We're at a *quick walk* for pace as everything has become so much more close-quartered.

About to turn the corner, we hear an enormous volley of rifle fire close by. There's shattering of glass and a man crying out. Briefly the shots stop, before erupting again. They are so close that I almost jump with each shot. Farra jukes his head around the corner and then shouts into his radio to stop firing. Following him round the corner, I see a limp figure on the floor, once a human but now a mangled wreck from the number of bullets that have ripped through his body.

"One more," I tell everyone and Farra indicates to move further down the hallway. As we walk past the window where all the bullets rained through, I get a cold shiver up my spine. My heart's thumping but I'm feeling cold and clammy at what I've seen.

There's a room to our left and Farra slides up to the door before quickly peeking in the small window. He gives a nod and we flank either side of the door. He steps across the front and is about to kick the door in when it comes off its hinges and he is driven back by the door and the crazed man behind it. They continue across the hallway and Farra is battered up against the wall.

Hughes reacts first and fires her shotgun at the man's legs, blowing a chunk off his knee cap area and he falls over as he turns. But he grabs my leg as he tumbles and it feels like a vice has gripped me. He bites into my leg and I feel him break the flesh. Hughes is butting her rifle into the man's face and he breaks off under constant attention.

He's a mess on the floor and he can't get any traction to stand, so I back off keeping myself clear. As the eyes look up at me, there's no recognition, just an anger, a hatred and I'm reminded of the eyes of the redhead. I'm almost in a trance looking at him when Hughes shouts a warning. It comes too late and I'm driven forward, hit by something in the back.

I roll forward and there's barking. Hughes cries out and I hear her fall to the ground. I've dropped my gun and am now on my back with a ravenous dog looking at me. It's a large Alsatian and he doesn't seem friendly, the same wild eyes that were in the men. It never dawned on me it could be used on animals.

As it approaches, slowly now awaiting my move, I am cornered and out of ideas. Hughes has fallen, and lies on the ground. I didn't see what happened but she's not moving. And then there's gunfire from behind me. The dog is twisted this way and that before bounding away round the corridor. And there comes the sniper fire we heard before, and I can only imagine the mess that the dog is now.

The man from the school room is dragging his way towards us and I see Gonzales grab Hughes' gun from the floor. He drives the butt into the man repeatedly until he stops moving. Only then does Kyla put down her gun and reach for me. I embrace her quickly but there's more to be done. We sweep into each room aware that we found one more crazy than we were expecting.

Looking back from a hot cup of coffee from the wagon feeding the multitude now on scene, we were lucky. In the classroom we never managed to get into, we found six children hiding in cupboards. In another room, three of Farra's men were holed up, bloodied and badly injured. But they were alive. Several didn't make it. And in another room we found the remaining kids and the rest of the SWAT team. The kids were silent but unharmed, the team were in need of serious medical attention.

Hughes was okay, stunned and sore. Farra had broken a few bones but was alive. I watch some of the parents seeing their kids for the first time after the ordeal and it does me good. Although one kid is crying to her mom, asking what was wrong with daddy.

Jenny Tattler's running the forensics and she makes a moment to come and see me. She throws her single arm around me and keeps saying "Thank God". I see Kyla's face as Jenny is holding me like more than a colleague. That's because she was and when times get bad, I guess she's a very close friend, or maybe a lover I just don't see anymore. Whatever, I'd be glad she was alive as well. When she leaves, Kyla wraps her arms around me and I feel like it's territory reaffirmed.

The Chief breaks up our moment. "Trimble, take a look at this. Forensics are checking the bodies inside but the crazies that we captured, all have a tattoo on the side of their necks. Both of the men have this. I have Tatler checking the corpses inside, including the dog. One has a tattoo of the school buildings but the other is of a child."

"I don't get it," says Kyla, "Who tattoos a school onto themselves? The child I get, a thing of affection but not this building."

"It's not affection, it's the mark. Sister Martha said there would be a mark of the target."

"But that meant..."

"Yeah Kyla, he meant to kill his child." And that's the most horrific thing I've seen or heard all day.

Chapter 17

Jenny Tattler's laying down all the reconstructed images they have found. The bodies had tattoos as well and although it took a bit of reproducing, they seemed to have managed it. There are four tattoos of the school, one of which was on the dog. But the other one was of a child. And that still haunts me, the implication he had targeted his own child. Two of the crazies are in hospital under special watch but they are not conscious.

"Can you tell if they are from the same artist?" asks Kyla. It's a good question.

"Everything indicates so, but we are still checking the inks to see if they match. But all the tattoos are very recent, inside of a week I would say, probably a lot less."

"Do we have to?" says Kyla looking at me. The others stare confused.

"Yes," I reply, "Off to see your favourite picture maker. Kyla's got a real thing for the guy we're going to see."

The others look bemused Kyla fills them in. "Trimble keeps company with some of the most odious people going, especially when it comes to tattoos."

"Jenny, give me some copies of those tattoos, I'll see if I can trace where they are coming from. Kyla, you're with me.

Gonzales, man the comms room, let me know if there's any reports right away. Hughes, get down the hospital, if those guys wake up I want to every bit of detail you can get out of them."

As Kyla drives the car downtown to the business premises of my favourite tattoo artist, I sit back for a moment in the car seat and find myself watching her. It was barely twenty four hours ago that I was believing she might not be alive and instead she's back to a fully functional Kyla. What also bothers me is how I am so accepting of the medical feat that's happened. This is not normal. Don't get me wrong, I'm delighted that Kyla's better, delighted that we can try to get more intimate, something her previous injuries prevented. But my view of life, of everything that makes up existence, is being jarred.

"I'm going to charge you by the hour for watching me."

"I'd take a year's subscription," I say and then we both laugh. "Sorry, that was so cheesy."

"Totally, but I can take it. Are you okay?"

"'Course not, Kyla. I'm doing my usual trick of delaying it all, pushing it back. I'll fall apart when this is all done."

"Okay, last night I just thought maybe you were hoping for more. Maybe you needed more. It's okay if you do, you can say."

"I was just happy to have you back, fully back. I reckoned on you being dead when she jabbed that doll. Whatever pace you want in this relationship is fine. I've pushed others too quick and got left with nothing."

"Jenny?" asks Kyla.

"Yeah, she was one. I don't want you to end up like her. Caring too much and having no true access."

Kyla nods and keeps driving. Maybe it's hard when someone

talks about their ex. My feelings for Jenny must show but I hope Kyla knows she's queen of this castle. She's also younger, and I don't want to be holding her back. She could do better than me.

"Just be straight with me," she says. "That's all I want. If you have needs, tell me. We'll make it work."

I place a hand upon her thigh and rub it gently.

"Is that all you need at the moment?" asks Kyla.

"No, but despite being a remarkable woman I doubt you could handle the car in this crosstown traffic with what I'm thinking." She punches my arm but the hand stays on her thigh.

We park a street away from the tattoo parlour and I see Kyla mentally prepare herself for Sketch's place. He's a damn fine tattoo artist but he's weird, perverted and weird. Last time he helped us, he was all over Kyla, despite her realising he kept tapes of female customers, especially those who needed tattoos in more private places.

I bang the door and hear the swearing from the back room. There's a brief delay until footsteps are heard inside and the door opens just a fraction.

"Not now. No, no, no. Not now, Trimble. You can't do this to me."

I place a foot in the door. "Right now. I ain't messing, Sketch, there are lives depending on me at the moment so open up."

"Okay, okay, can you give me ten minutes, maybe fifteen and I'll be done. Have a client inside, you see. We kinda need space."

I push the door firmly and force him backwards. He swears but then flashes a smile at Kyla. Ignoring him, I walk on past him towards the rear room where he does his work. There's a cry behind me telling me to hold up but it's too late. Opening the door to the rear suite, I am confronted by the bare behind of a girl. Whilst hardly being repulsed, I turn away as the girl seems rather young.

"Kyla, go through there and make sure Sketch's guest is decent, if you would." Kyla brushes past me and I eye Sketch up. He can probably tell my mood as my nostrils are starting to flare. I hear the girl complain that the portrait wasn't complete and how was she going to get her big start without it.

"Sketch," I say, "I'm going to check her age and ID, and if she's not legal, I will break your face. I will then call her father and let Kyla hand him the meat clever to remove your private parts with."

"Come on, Trimble, like I would." But he's quaking underneath.

"It's okay, you can come in," calls Kyla. On entering the room, I see a blonde girl, wrapped in a blanket, and her face looks so young. I may just be an old fart but I need to make sure.

"She says that Sketch took her clothing, putting it somewhere safe while he did the sketch for the movie men." Kyla's looking at Sketch, her eyebrows raised.

"Okay, it can be distracting when you're drawing. Look!" He pulls down a rolled up screen at the doors and it shows a wilderness landscape. Kyla spins an easel round and it shows the same picture but with a naked girl. The facial detail is stunning but the image is highly provocative. I'm guessing he was nearing the end of the sitting and ready for special payment, the dirty john.

Sketch pops the backdrop back up into its roll. "Her clothes are here in the cupboard." Sketch hands Kyla the clothing and I then direct him back out of the room. He seems indignant as I guess he's been looking at this girl for the last couple of hours but he's getting no more pleasure.

A few minutes later Kyla comes through the door. She walks right up to Sketch and pushes him back against a wall, putting her face right into his.

"What age is she, Sketch?"

He looks panicked. "She said she was legal, said it was all okay. I mean she was in a bar when we met. She must have been legal."

"Look at her, Sketch, does she look eighteen? Does she? I mean, you've had a full all over look so you must be able to guess."

"I don't know. But she said she was."

Kyla turns to me. "She's Mila Fordyce, a student up at the university, and she's been eighteen for at least four weeks. But that dirty sod didn't even ask." Kyla turned back to Sketch. "And when did you become a major agent for the movie studios. And who does paintings to star in the movies. I have ordered a taxi, Sketch, which you will pay for her, and you'll also give her that painting to take away and payment for her time modelling for you. Otherwise I will find stuff to book you for."

She turns on her heel and walks back into the rear room. I hear her giving the girl a lecture about not being gullible and stupid, and not having sex with *greasy, dirty minded, perverts that only want to take women for what they can give to his organ.* Sketch shifts uneasily as he hears this. I just smile.

With the girl gone, we take Sketch into the back room and sit him down with the sketches from Jenny Tatler. He's adamant it's not his work, even offering to let us see his videos of clients to make sure.

"Whose work is it, Sketch? Does it look familiar?" I ask.

"The face could be anyone. It's not like it's an impression piece or stylized. It's a dead straight portrait. But the cityscape is familiar. There's a guy on the Southside who draws like that. But he's into weird stuff."

"Weird stuff. You think he's into weird stuff?" asks Kyla.

"Oh he is. Seriously weird. I might draw my creatures and place them into fantasy scenes, or even have them on an arm. But this guy takes creatures and people and makes them do all sorts of stuff."

"Like what?"

"Well, like what a man and a woman would do, except it's a creature or animal. It's pretty gross and full on. Like a porno of the animal kingdom. Actually animals don't look this gross doing it."

"Got a name?" I ask.

"He's known as AC. I don't know his real name."

"Why AC?"

"Anti-Christ. There's seriously black stuff in his collection, the church doesn't come out very well in his drawings."

"And you know him, how?"

"Purely from reputation, and having seen a few of his drawings once. I walked from them. That's how bad it was, I actually walked, Trimble."

"Address?"

"Try 3rd and Elm in Edelweiss. I'm not sure of the building but it was down there. And Trimble, you got none of this from me. I ain't getting into that sort of trouble. He's bad news."

"Okay Sketch, you've been very helpful. And remember, I can't stop girls being stupid and coming here but you damn well check their age."

He nods and I get up. On my way out I sweep a look around

the room, seeing the generous number of pictures on the wall. Although, he's often a bit strange and fantastical in his work, it is stunning. The women look fantastic, even if they actually would be very cold in that sort of clothing. And then one picture catches my eye.

It's a young woman, brunette hair blowing in the wind. She sports a huge sword above her head as she is fighting a beast. But aside for bracelets, ankle bands and strangely enough, gauntlets, she seems under protected. Her figure is stunning and possibly slightly better than the original. But then no woman ever looked like that. But the face is spot on.

"Corstain, there's one of you here." I walk away. From the sounds of it, I think she grabbed him down below and applied serious pressure. She may also have kicked him there. And then there was the ripping of the paper off the wall.

Chapter 18

3rd and Elm is not a great district to be in and I call for back up to sit a few streets back. Heavy back up, the one with automatic weapons. But the mood is light in the car on the way over, Kyla still smarting from the picture on Sketch's wall.

"Look at that. The cheeky bastard, I mean drawing me in the buff, stood like that."

"I know," I say, "you would catch cold."

"Oi, I don't need some sarcasm from you. I need reaffirming here. I need to hear that he's a disgusting letch."

"He is. But he's also a damn good artist. Your face is stunning, he's even got that gritted teeth thing you do when angry."

"What gritted teeth thing?"

"That one. Hey, don't give me those eyes. It's a good look. You are something else and he's captured your face incredibly well."

"And the rest of it. You're okay with him drawing me like that?"

"Of course not. He's got no right, I'm just saying it's a good drawing. If you had wanted it, it would have been a really good job. You didn't and that's not right."

"Thank you."

"Still looks great though. Would have been better with your

real body though."

"You think so? You think my body's better than that?"

I sigh. This is going to be awkward and territory I shouldn't have got myself into. "No one's body is better than that. There isn't a woman whose body looks like that. We all have little marks and that. Nobody is perfect."

"Gee, thanks. You could have just blagged it."

"No. Because your body is amazing. And it's real. I'll take real over this fake stuff any day. But not if he's going to draw it."

She's looking at me, assessing if I am genuine. I am. Why can't women just accept it when we're genuine? She asks to keep it real, I do and she's not happy. Oh well, not a lot I can do about that.

"Anyway, we play this next bit cool, okay? We don't know what this guy has or hasn't?"

"Okay. But you know that the cavalry may not be enough. Sometimes it's not guns we need."

"I know," I say, "But Sister Martha seems to be keeping a wide berth. She doesn't exactly leap to the fore with me. It's a coded word every now and then."

"I know but..."

The car swerves and I grab the wheel, keeping us on the road. There are hoots from horns but I'm just keen to keep us moving in a straight line.

"Kyla! Kyla! Can we pull over?"

Her eyes flash at me and she seems desperate but manages to let off the throttle and we pull into the side of the road. She's sweating, eyes looking at the dashboard. I take her hand and she clutches me.

"What? What's up?" I ask.

"I saw him. I saw the Darkness. He was…, it was disgusting."

"Where were you?"

"In a room, with an artist's easel. And I was painting and there was a woman and him. Doing…, I can't picture it, I won't picture it."

"Okay, ease down. We'll walk from here, it's only round the corner. Are you okay, or should I get Hughes?"

The teeth are gritted. "No, I'm good. Let's go sort this." And that is damn sexy. Determined and focused, I can't help but get excited by her look when she's this way. But maybe I won't tell her right now.

The streets are pretty quiet and I try not to look out of place but really, this place is for weirdos. I know I'm not being very politically correct but I'm sorry, everything is weird here to me. Dress, sex, desires, just so foreign to me. I don't mean those of different orientation or those struggling to know who they are. This is not that. This is actually freakish.

A couple walk past us and I really don't know what style or look they are going for. It beats me. But I can see the knife being carried and no doubt there's a firearm there if things get messy. I keep eyes focused away, not too far lest they think me an easy picking. But far enough away.

"Tattoo parlour, over the road," says Kyla.

"Sense anything from it?"

"Not that one."

"Okay, we carry on. See if there are any more further down."

We walk on and I can see Kyla struggling as we walk past a building indicating money transfer. Continuing past I pull her into a side street and pull her close. I place my hands inside her jacket pretending to fondle her but whisper "in there?"

She whispers "yes" and lets me break off. The shop front is

awash with posters and you cannot see anything inside. I push the door and am hit by a fusty smell. Kyla's head is hung low and I reckon she's sensing a lot. I turn to her and advise her to look like she's been drugged. There's a raise of the eyes before she drops into character.

A man, of possibly Eastern European heritage, sits behind a desk and looks me up and down. I drag Kyla over and place an arm round her.

"Not a bad piece, don't you think?" I hold Kyla's cheek and then push her away. "But to business. I'm here for the removals."

The man looks at me. For a moment he thinks about what I've said, looks at Kyla and then indicates with a flick of his head that I should go into the back. Smiling, I grab Kyla's arm and push her on ahead of me. She makes a good show of stumbling along.

There's a short corridor and then we are in a room with red drapes and the smell of drugs and alcohol. A white man sits there, and beckons me forward, leaning forward so I can bend down to him.

"I'm here about the removals. Got my ticket with me," I say, indicating Kyla.

"He's in a sitting at the moment. Important client, might be a while. You can wait or just leave the girl. I'll entertain her until you come back."

There's a door that reads *private* beyond us and I wonder what's best. I'm hardly going to leave Kyla on her own but just sitting around, being plied with drugs and alcohol isn't going to work either. A glance at Kyla shows me she's agitated and not just playing her character. Her hand has a finger pointing at the door. Then there's a scream. It's a woman's scream, and it chills me. I've heard many screams in my time. Some are people screaming at something, some are people who are just afraid. Others are people who think they are going to die. This is in the last category.

I throw a punch at the man, knocking him back and follow with two more, making sure he's out. Kyla's kicking the door as the man from the front comes in with a gun. I draw and shoot him in the shoulder, causing him to drop his gun. I press the button on my phone that calls for backup. The GPS will direct them. Then I follow Kyla in through the door.

I never freeze, never. But the tableau before me causes me to shake. Six feet away is the demon I saw when they tried to kill me. And it's doing something I can't begin to describe to a poor girl. I fire the gun but it won't fire. And the creature laughs.

Chapter 19

There's real panic building inside me and I simply run at the demon. With a swish of its hand, I find myself sailing through the air, crashing into the wall of the room. The floor arrives quickly too and I struggle to lift myself up. As I manage to get to my knees, someone kicks me in the gut. The wind is knocked out of me and I have to fight hard to keep going. Before lifting myself, I swing an arm out and find a leg to hold onto.

I may give out an image as an upright and fine police detective but when it comes to my life, I fight dirty with the best of them. I pull myself towards the leg and bite it hard. There's a shout and I keep my purchase but move my left hand up the leg until I find the genitals. And I damn well squeeze.

My attacker is stunned enough for me to rise and I pummel him with a punch. He's covered in tattoos, right across the whole body and I notice a few upside down crosses amongst the artwork.

Kyla screams. Turning, I see her in the air, about a foot off the ground, floating towards the demon who still has the other woman in his grasp. Kyla sails over at break neck speed and is engulfed by an arm. He is over her neck, drooling some sort of fluid, like a letch with saliva issues.

What do I do? The gun didn't work last time. But he isn't looking at me. So where's the gun? I can't see it. I need a weapon. Grabbing the easel, I charge at the demon who is engrossed in Kyla. With everything I've got I crash into it, easel between us. Everyone falls, everyone tumbles down.

There's noise outside, gunfire. The demon is rising and I grab Kyla and roll her out of the way. My back's up against a wall and I don't know what to do when it makes its next move on us. There's no gun nearby.

The room explodes in noise and light. My ears ring and my senses are scrambled. I can't see anything, there's just a gong going off repeatedly in my ears, drowning out all other sounds. I cling to Kyla. A man in a mask grabs me and looks me over before leaving me.

Slowly my eyes are able to see the whole room, flooded with SWAT team members. Groggily, I get to my feet and see a SWAT team member going through a door I hadn't seen before. I follow, falling off the walls of the narrow corridor several times. The corridor ends in bright sunshine and I find myself partially blinded. Turning a corner, I am in a back alley and there are SWAT team members further up, trying to search for someone.

I'm exhausted and still have poor hearing due to the ringing from the flashbang. The team seem to be going well covering the street and I rest up in a doorway, thankful for being alive. And then the door I'm leaning on gives way.

I drop like a bag of potatoes onto a concrete floor and two arms pull me inside. Leaning over me is a red hooded woman whose eyes I have seen before. I go to reach up but find only a hand to my face which scratches my cheek deep.

I hear the door close and the light is gone, leaving only a

dimness. She turns around and straddles me and I see one arm go behind her and feel something metallic pushed at my genitals.

"Scream and I will castrate you in the fastest way possible." There's hellfire in her eyes and she almost seems to be getting off on inflicting this pain. "He says your woman felt good. Says he wants her. And I'll have you. Trimble, join us. Stop being our enemy and join us. You can have any woman you choose, or I'll make you a police chief, or even mayor. With me, you can have everything."

Looking up, her face seems manic, but her body is one seductive curse. The hooded robe is designed to pretend it's covering everything but it's showing me all a man wants to see. She's exciting the raw animal beneath and she knows it. Power and domination, a toxic brew that flows to my mind.

But I left someone behind in the room. And it's her that comes to mind now. With every bit of effort I can muster I draw a load of spit in my mouth and launch it into her face. "You can keep your damn women and promotions. Go back to hell."

"You haven't seen hell yet, Trimble. When it's unleashed, it'll tear this place apart. When they all drink from the cup, when vengeance is sought, it'll make the school look like a kids' science experiment. But you'll be singing in a higher pitch."

The door bursts open and she's away like a whippet, her robed figure disappearing over me. But she's left her mark and I feel the blood from her scratch trickle to my mouth. The face of a masked woman leans over me. Briefly she drops it and I see a taught face, much younger than me, but showing an intensity and asking if I am alright. After what was before me, it's a beautiful face but I really shouldn't have said that out loud.

Getting to my feet, I look around for the redhead but she's gone. The SWAT team operative with the beautiful face says they are all gone. So I make my way back to where Kyla was and find her wrapped in a silver blanket, shaking. Across the room lies the naked body of the girl we saw with the demon. There's no artist and no demon.

"He touched me," says Kyla.

"I know," I say trying to comfort.

"No Mulgrew, he touched me." This time she opens the blanket slightly and I can see her top is ripped wide open. I kiss her forehead and reach down to grab either side of her leather jacket and zip it up. Taking the foil off her shoulders, I grab her hand and lead her out of the building.

There's a ton of forensics to be done here. We may even get some leads. But right now I need a nun who cannot see. And she needs to tell me how I fight a demon. Because we got lucky. We got very lucky.

Chapter 20

Sister Martha arrives in a squad car and has a young girl with her, seemingly leading her to the building which I stand in front of. Inside the building, O'Halloran is conducting forensics in his usual morbid way. And Kyla is fronting up as best she can. She's co-ordinating the surrounding area search with Hughes but there's a real edge to her I haven't seen before. I think they woke the lion.

"Detective Trimble," announces Sister Martha, shocking a few of the uniforms who are wondering how a nun with no eyes knew I was there. "It seems you are getting close."

"Not close enough. And not in a clever way either. Come inside and talk, I need your wisdom."

The girl leads Sister Martha inside the building and we are in the front room where it all began. The man who was on the counter is dead, double tapped by the SWAT team when they raided. There's also a bullet hole in his shoulder as I don't shoot the way the team do.

"It was here?"

"Yes Sister, two rooms through. It had a girl with it and was being painted or sketched doing things it shouldn't with her. She's now dead. O'Halloran says her neck was snapped."

The Sister is visibly affected. "Poor girl. But you and

Corstain came out?"

"Barely. And it touched Kyla, grabbed her, felt her..., her..."

"I'm a nun, not your mother, you can say boobs."

I have said much worse to my mother when she was alive. It's just that Martha's a nun and I find discussing anything sexual with a nun somewhat disturbing. I know, but it's the upbringing.

"How did you get out?" asks Sister Martha.

"I hit it with an artist's easel. I think it was too engrossed in Kyla and the other girl. I also ran into our red headed friend from before. She stuck a gun between my legs and threatened to blow my future family to kingdom come. But not before she asked me to join her."

Martha nodded. "You are a main player, affecting things. They will offer the world to have your submission. And this red head, she is offering you herself, sex, power and anything you want." I nod. "Be careful. She will be enticing. You have a base instinct and it's not a bad thing but with women as deep in the dark things as her, it can be held to ransom. And I see she has marked you, right there on the cheek. Be very careful, I think she wants you for herself."

"The demon threw me across the room with a sweep of his hand, and then he made Kyla float to him. How do we combat that? How do we stop it?"

Sister Martha sits down with a sigh on an old armchair. "I didn't think it would manifest in such a physical form. I'll get some things to help you but you're not going to be able to pass them around everyone. You can't kill it, so to speak, but you can destroy this physical manifestation. There are weapons but I need to go to our quartermaster, we don't carry such precious items around with us."

O'Halloran barges in from the rear room, shouting at me.

"Trimble, the girl that died, there's a tattoo on the side of her neck. It's been slightly disfigured but we've got a partial recognition on the face. It belongs to Geraint Jones, apparently of 1345 Danver Way in the ..."

"Expensive side of town. Jones, purveyor of high class hookers. No wonder she wanted to take the cup and kill him. But he runs a tight leash on them. We might be able to get movements. Any other interesting items?"

O'Halloran shakes his head. "Nothing definite yet. We're trying to get some prints or hairs so we can get a trace on your artist. And as for your demon, it's like it was never there."

I nod and turn back to the Sister who seems deep in thought. "Did the red head say anything else to you?"

"Only that when they all drink from the cup we would see hell. It was all very vague. The thing is if we got a lot of people all entranced from this blood chalice at the same time, I don't know if we could handle it. We have to almost remove the head to stop them."

"Yes, they become like savages, zombies almost with just a goal of destruction on the one they are marked with. Removing the head would indeed stop them, but there is another way Detective. Remove the mark."

"What? Just cut a bit of flesh off."

"Better than losing your head, don't you think?"

I pick up the mobile and ring Gonzales, asking him to get to the hospital and advise the doctors to remove the tattoos on our sedated attackers from the school. Then I wave Sister Martha off and agree to meet her later for a weapons rendezvous.

Everything is running well at the scene and I turn over the

operation to Hughes and seek out Kyla. I find her sitting on the ground outside a coffee stall. Sitting down next to her, I put my arm around her.

"Are you okay? Do you want to talk...?"

"Shut up and just hold me. You have no idea what that was like."

"Hey, my knackers were held up with a gun."

She laughs. And I shut up.

Chapter 21

I'm not a big fan of hospitals. The people there do some great work and they usually put heart and soul into it. But despite that, I find my recent hospital experiences to be somewhat strange and unpleasant. Kyla lost the use of her legs when we were at the hospital. My mother died in a hospital. Oh yeah, I watched a woman float, fly out of a window and walk her broken body into the hospital incinerator. They don't provide feedback forms for that.

But thanks to Sister Martha, we have a chance at questioning two of the people who have been turned into raging crazies. I know it's not a medical term but "crazies" is about the right amount of madness and accuracy we need for what happens to them. The doctor I saw said another word but I never did Latin at school.

Our two crazies are in an isolated wing of the hospital, some twenty floors up. It seemed best from a security point of view and until very recently they have been kept sedated. Even now, having had the tattoos cut from their skin, they are still restrained by some of the strongest binds I have seen in a hospital. Outside their rooms, armed police keep watch.

From outside the rooms, I watch one of the crazies being woken up from his drug induced sleep. There's a moment of thrashing as the doctor places a needle into the man's arm but the restraints hold and gradually he settles down before his eyes suddenly flick open. He seems terrified and starts to sweat profusely. Pumping some more drugs into him, the doctor seems pleased enough when the man remains alert. We are waved in.

Kyla's taking the lead on this, and I'll just watch from the back of the room. After everything they've been through, I believe our crazies would benefit from a good looking face and a sweet voice. As I lean against the wall, I watch Kyla take a hair tie and wrap her brunette mop behind her, exposing the neck that first took me. She takes off her leather jacket and I enjoy the taught body as she walks to the bedside. *Come on Kyle, time to be professional.*

"John? John? It's okay. You're in hospital, it's all over. All done John. You're safe."

The man looks around him, still agitated. He looks beyond Kyla, at me, at the guards outside and then stares at the doctor. It's almost like he's checking out a new body and how it works. His fingers unfurl and then form a clasp again. His legs move a fraction, held by the restraints, but under the sheet I swear he's flexing newly found toes.

"Your son, John, he's okay. You didn't go through with it."

"He's not my son," spits the man.

I guess technically he isn't. He's a stepson we found out. A stepson of five years.

"He's alive, John. Why did you want him dead?"

The man looks at Kyla like she's asked the daftest and most simple question imaginable. "He gets in the way. Everywhere we go, he has to be there, has to be with Mom. Go somewhere nice and he's spoiling it. Won't stay with anyone else so we don't get any time. And when she's pleasing me, I hear the footsteps. Little shit comes banging on the door. She won't even finish me off before going to him. And that's it for that night. Little shit gets in the way."

I'm not a parent, not even a person who finds children adorable and cute, but even I'm thinking we should have just blown this guy away. It does take the sting away from a father hunting his own son. But the hatred is astonishing against such a young child. Frustration is one thing, wanting to kill the kid, that's just plain evil.

"Where did you go? How did you find out about the chalice?" He seems bemused. "The cup?"

"Do I get something for this?" he asks, plainly quite lucid now. "I mean you're going to lock me up."

"It'll help. Maybe you might see the sun one day," says Kyla, holding a dispassionate voice. The man's assessing her, not just what she's saying but also physically. She looks like she's not even bothered by his lecherous eyes but I reckon deep down she wants to smack him. I know I do.

"Why not? It was that bitch's fault anyway. My shrink told me to go to a place. 3rd and Elm. That was the street."

Outside the door I overhear one of the guards' radios saying something about a disturbance.

"And you were tattooed there?"

"Yes," says the former crazy. "But not before I did that hobo in. They pointed him out, said he was just unlucky in life. Was remarkably easy. Waste of space anyway. Wasn't like he'd be missed."

"What's your shrink's name?"

"Lowenstein. Nice legs but her top half ain't as good as yours."

Kyla doesn't flinch. "First name?"

"Tania. Posh bird. You could learn a lot from her. She wasn't unwilling to help in deep, healing ways. I reckon you could heal me."

The radio outside is alive with lots of fast chatter I can't make out. I see one of the seniors in the guard troop coming down the corridor, indicating he needs through in a hurry.

"So you went with her idea because she let you have her? Bit weak, don't you think?"

"Hey, she didn't let me, I took her. She couldn't resist."

The senior guard comes into the room and whispers in my ear.

"Sorry sir but we need to move these guys. The morgue has been emptying. Bodies just getting up and walking out. All getting to the elevators and stairs. I've shut down the elevators but there's movement on the stairs. They seem to be coming this way. Dead bodies! They are walking this way."

Our crazy suddenly seems less sure about himself and I notice Kyla flinch like she did in the car near 3rd and Elm. Her look confirms what I need to know.

"Okay, get this man up. And you," I say to the senior guard, "get next door and take the man in there under your protection. Get him in a wagon and rendezvous at headquarters, we can defend them better there."

He nods and leaves the room. Kyla and a somewhat bemused doctor start unstrapping the man but it takes time due to the extra bonds he's secured with. Outside, I hear a panic in the corridor. A quick glance and I see dead people, full naked with tags on their toes, walking down the corridor. One of them has a nurse in their arms, gripping her tight. She's screaming.

"Take them down, don't hesitate," I cry.

The radio of the guards is squawking and I overhear my name. "Tell Trimble, there's something climbing up the outside wall, several of them. Like spiders, all heading towards your floor!"

Chapter 22

"Kyla, something's going to come through that window! Just get the bed moving, we'll shoot our way out."

I put my head out through the door and tell the guards to open fire. They're reluctant as behind the dead bodies is an open corridor and there are hospital staff running around still. I yell to clear the corridor but the bodies are closing in fast.

A cacophony of gunfire begins and the reanimated bodies begin to fall apart. But they keep moving. Arms fall off, bits of long dead flesh drop. One loses a leg and then still tries to drag itself along the corridor.

The nurse in the grasp of the body screams, yelling not to shoot her. But the bodies are getting close and the guards break rank to tackle them hand to hand. The first guard takes a flinging arm and falls to the ground. Others are grabbed by cold hands. And then the corpse at the centre carrying the nurse stops and sets her down gently. She smiles at me, licking her lips in a sensual manner as she places a finger to them. "Hello Mulgrew, want to handle me again?"

I look to draw my own weapon as she removes her nurse's hat and shakes out the long red hair. But a corpse grabs my arm and I punch hard at its chin. But all I get is a sore hand

and am pushed back through the door to the room where our interview was being held.

There's a crash at the windows and small black creatures, the size of a human head, scuttle into the room. They have legs like a spider, long and thin, but there must be at least twenty legs. One jumps onto the bed and Kyla grabs it from behind, automatically flinging it across the room. She's drawn her gun and shoots another as it moves across the wall. Black blood like goo splatters everywhere.

"Kyla!"

My warning is too late as Kyla is grabbed from behind by the red head. She holds Kyla's ponytail in one hand, pulling her head back and has an arm around her, gripping her tight.

"He says he's not finished with you. Next time he wants it all." She sniffs the air in a gross reference. The black creatures are now jumping all over our crazy and he is ripped from his bonds by them. I hear bones break as the bonds don't fail but instead his body is twisted and shattered in its removal. He should be screaming but one of the black creatures covers his face.

"Long way down, Trimble," says the red head and then she looks at our crazy. He's suddenly catapulted through the window and glass explodes. The redhead follows across the room dragging Kyla. "Maybe we should get rid of my competition. Don't worry, he'll soon forget you when he's having me all night." She pulls Kyla's face right back and then brings her face close to Kyla so she can see the wildness in the eyes.

The eyes entrance me but Kyla just looks pissed. And she strains as hard as she can, momentarily breaking the hold on her hair as the woman's hand slips off. Kyla bites hard into her face. The red head releases her grasp and holds her face and Kyla follows up with a kick to the midriff. She's about to go in with more punches when she's grabbed by a corpse from behind.

"Next time, I'll just snap her neck," cries the red head. Kyla's fighting hard against the corpse but she just can't reach. "Next time, Mulgrew." And the red head runs to the window and throws herself out of it.

I'm kicking hard against the corpse that holds me when I see the black creatures all start to race out through the window. In thirty seconds they are gone. There's more commotion in the hallway and more guards arrive outside and start to pepper the corpses in the corridor with bullets from behind.

And then the corpses just fall to the ground, slipping off whoever they are holding, or just simply collapsing to the deck. I race to the broken window and look for her but the red head is gone. On the ground are two bodies, separated by a distance. One is the man I saw being flung out of the window. He is joined on the ground by the other crazy from the adjacent suite.

Kyla disappears into the corridor shouting, "Stand down" to everyone. It's a bizarre scene, old dead bodies that had just been attacking us lie on the ground beside some fresh ones. Some of the guards are moaning in pain and Kyla's shouting for medical help. Even despite this madness, I hear medical professionals running to our assistance.

Soon our wounded and dead are being taken care of and I am able to step away from the scene, still fighting to comprehend what I saw. The black creatures and the way she controlled them, the dead rising and her eyes, the red head holding Kyla in her grasp. She could have killed her. Why didn't she?

Maybe she wasn't allowed to. Maybe that demon wants her for himself. The thought chills me.

I find Kyla in the hospital cafeteria, trying to eat a tuna mayo sandwich but she doesn't seem that enthusiastic. There's a plastic cup of what probably approximates to coffee, and it's untouched. Her hair is down from its ponytail. Her eyes are red and there's still some water in them, the last few remaining tears.

"You okay?"

"Hardly," she sniffs. "What is it with her? Why does she want you? And why didn't she just kill me? You were being held, we were right in it. She had no need to give me that opening. And even then she didn't act."

"Guess we were lucky," I say, not wanting to weigh her down further with morbid ideas.

"Bull, Mulgrew, total bull. Don't placate me. I don't need being treated with kid gloves. It was because he wants me. That thing wants another go."

"Why are you so sure? Sure, it crossed my mind but why so positive?"

"When he held me, when he ripped my top and..., well frankly, groped me, it was more than disgusting, more than an invasion. Ever since, I can feel him."

I nod. "There's bound to be memories coming back to you of it. Rape victims have that. Maybe you need to talk to someone professional."

Her fist slams the table spilling the coffee. "Don't you get it? It's not in my mind, it's real, like he's permanently doing it over and over again. Like we're conjoined."

The cafeteria is silent. I doubt they can even grasp what she is on about but there are no wise cracks. If there was, I'm not sure which of us would get to the person first.

In a lower voice she says, "He's where that special person in your life should be. He's where you should be."

I gulp a little at that. I knew we were close but that is something she's never said. She's shaking now but trying to hold it together.

"When my legs failed, it was awful but there was nothing else, just no feeling. And I even managed to reconcile myself to a life like that, one where I couldn't enjoy a full relationship because of the paralysis. And then it was all up for grabs again. But now, he's with me everywhere. If I shower, it's like he's in with me. And meantime, his bitch is giving you a come on which makes me want to compete, to drop to her sordid level of attraction."

My mind's confused. How do you deal with this? There's no manual, no self-help book for demonic influences trying to break up a relationship. Actually maybe there is but what do they know?

"We need to see the Sister about this. She might have something that'll help. They cured Hughes that time she got hit with the dart. And your legs!"

She looks crestfallen. "I was hoping my knight might have had something to lift me up with." She gets up and starts to walk away. I see her hair tie still on the table.

"Kyla," I shout after her. Turning, she scowls at me as I approach. With slightly trembling hands, aware that I need to deliver some magic touch, I reach round and gather her hair up, forming the ponytail and then securing it. But I hold it there, focusing on her neck, letting my face betray that feeling I get every time she does this action to herself.

"Why..."

"Because sometimes it can feel like I'm just a dirty john, staring. You had me at the train station, stood there with no luggage and a formal handshake. A shake of that hair and then, that neck."

She kisses my cheek and then looks into my eyes. "Martha." There's a resolution in the voice.

"Martha," I say. And then we both go red, embarrassed as hell when a ripple of applause and whoop whooping noises break out from a watching cafe. I think my life jumped into the wrong novel.

Chapter 23

Kyla takes the wheel as we drive over to the cathedral, hoping that Sister Martha has something for us, something we can battle this foe with. The Chief calls for an update, complaining that he has to handle press conference after press conference. "And how much of what happened in the hospital do I let out? Who saw what? There are tales of drones with legs entering the building."

I wish I had answers for the guy but that's his job, I need to find the source of all this, find the chalice and put a stop to the whole thing. In that vein, I call Gonzales and ask if he can track down Tania Lowenstein, the shrink that got my crazy into this whole business. I'm thinking it might be a dead end but I'm not sure if it will be a body or just no evidence.

Kyla seems more focused and she even tunes the radio station in to a channel she wants. Normally she won't touch it if it's on, letting me have my music. But at the moment she's swinging along to a rock track. Suits her too. Although Gonzales was a bit surprised when he caught it on the phone.

When we enter the cathedral, there's already a young girl waiting for us who leads us directly to the Sister's cell. It's bloody disturbing when that happens, as if to remind you that you are entering the presence of someone who knows all. Of course she would say that's Him, and not herself at all.

"It is good to see you both still standing." That still sounds weird from a nun with no eyes. "I heard about the hospital incident. You are getting to them, an open attack with creatures from the dark. The creature, the demon would rather lurk in the shadows, have the world believe it is all a man-made hell but you are forcing his hand. It would have been easy to kill the unfortunates in the school, but you spared them where you could. Mercy wins ground. Do you see?"

I'm not wholly sure you can assess the school incident that positively but I'm not here to argue. "Have you got any way for us to fight the demon? We can't get near it and I doubt corporeal items like bullets will do much."

"Ah," says the Sister, "Don't forget corporeal things do have an effect. It can be struck although the effects will not hold for long. So by all means, *tag it*. That's how you put it, yes? But to take it down you will need this."

Walking over to a small casket on the floor by her rudimentary bed, she bends down and snaps the container open. From within, she removes a long thin item wrapped in cloths, which she brings to her bed. Unfolding the cloths reveals a long and thin knife.

"You will not read about this knife anywhere. There is no official church record of it and yet it has been used before to send this particular demon back to the ethereal realm. Be warned, it will recognise it and may even sense it from a distance. But you need to stab the demon with it. In the chest. Around the heart area would be good."

"Just a knife?" asks Kyla.

"The handle is carved from wood that sustained an ancient site in the Middle East, a most blessed area in its day. The blade was consecrated for this purpose by a third generation descendant of Peter, the church's rock. At least that's the legend. The handle part is true though and its effectiveness is assured."

"What about the redhead?" asks Kyla.

"What about her?" snaps the Sister, "The demon is the main head, do not be distracted by this toy that it chooses to use. The demon and the chalice must be stopped. It will be no use stopping her if these others fail." Kyla looks a bit pissed at the comments.

I recount what has been happening with the redhead and how she has been trying to turn me, make me a toy. That leads into Kyla's incident with the demon and how she is still feeling his effects, particularly how the demon seems to be touching her intimately although it's not even in the room.

"They are scared of you. Both of you. This is good for they are seeking to break you up. The feeling of its touch, that sickening invasion it has made will not be stopped until you destroy its corporeal form. The knife will be your way out. As for her interest in you detective Trimble, it is to take you off the case, to push you away from your partner. It isn't difficult to see you have feelings for each other. They seek to exploit any weakness there. Be careful.

"When it came to the city, when you stopped the massacres, I fought it with a number of us, one being Father Krystanovic. We shared a lot as friends, as brother and sister in the faith. And yet he died believing I had betrayed him due to the demon's images and twists. It is a deceiver and a liar. Beware for it will twist how you see each other."

Taking our leave of the Sister, I get a call from Gonzales with an address for the shrink's office and we proceed to the high class office near the city centre. Kyla finds a car park a few blocks away as we don't want to be seen as having discovered something lest they close the lead we find before we can follow them.

The office is at the top of a tall skyscraper. It seems a little strange that a shrink should have the entire top floor but when we arrive, we find that the building has many offices boarded up for a rat infestation problem. I ring the office and they get hold of city to clarify. There is indeed a rat problem and no amount of effort has shifted them.

There are sixty-four floors in this sky scraper and I risk the lift to get to the top floor. The building seems deserted and we ride to the top floor without incident but there's an eerie feel to the structure. The doors open and reveal a stylish set of offices as well as a reception suite. Everything looks like a working office except there's no one there.

"We need to see if anyone has been coming in or out of here," says Kyla. "The whole place just seems too lived in."

We enter the main office, which is unlocked, and it leads to a smart room with a sofa, table and relaxing chairs. It has a view of the city that is incredible, the walls consisting of just windows on two sides.

"So this is where she got into their heads," I say. But there's nothing that looks unusual. Kyla walks through a side door and shouts back that she's found the kitchen. I take a look at the books on the table of what would be Lowenstein's personal secretary. One says diary on it and I wonder why the place isn't locked up, like the diary should be.

Opening the diary I find the last entry, made yesterday. It says *"Sent home at 1453 due to private meeting with Lady Sankoule."* I wonder who this is. It's not a name I've seen so far in our investigations at any point.

Then I hear Kyla scream. She barges through the door and promptly vomits onto the floor. I smell death in the other room and something else. There's a screeching and something like chewing. I help Kyla by slapping her back, clearing her stomach. But she's white, pure white from what she saw.

"Mulgrew, there's a woman in the fridge, parts of..., dear God, she's..."

Kyla can't go on. I rush into the next room and look at the open fridge door. There are rats and a woman. But she's in too many pieces and they are just ravenous.

Chapter 24

"Are we going about this the right way?"

I look at Kyla. She's still white from what she saw. "How do you mean?"

"Every time we are behind the drag curve, every time arriving just too late. There's a kill order out for innocents. But this means lots of individual murders, hard to police but surely slow in numbers. I mean, we have been scouring what's going on and there's been a few but it's hardly been chaos."

I shake my head. "I don't follow. Are you saying we haven't been busy enough?"

"Exactly."

"But I've been off my feet. We haven't stopped."

Kyla shakes her head, "We've been looking for the needle in the haystack. What's the goal here? They will want to take over the city. How do you do that? It's a demon with a body. So it will want an empire. It seems to have needs, a need to humiliate, to destroy in a sexual or physical sense. It wants to rule. There's an end game we are not seeing, Mulgrew. Why manifest yourself if not to rule in the physical world? And ruling means land, means owning, and means running a place for your benefit."

"What benefit can it take?"

"Bedlam. Hell is bedlam, is it not? It wants a city in chaos, an affront to all good things. So what's the big play?"

I look dumbly at her. I'm not getting it.

"We dealt with three at the school. That was messy. But imagine hundreds rampaging like that. I think they are experimenting at the moment. The real destruction is to come.

Kyla shivers and clutches her hands to her chest. When she said she felt him, I thought it was like I feel if it's dark and I'm in a bad memory. That crawling skin feeling. But I see her actually feeling like she's being touched, across that which she holds intimate. I'm not sure I can comprehend the hell that is.

O'Halloran approaches. I'm always happier to see Jenny Tatler but O'Halloran is a quality scenes of crime officer yet even he looks a little off. There's a paleness in his complexion that is rarely seen.

"Can you not follow normal people for a change? When it started it was a hung up priest but now you give me chopped women in a fridge, stored with the fruit juice. She was tortured as well. If you got a look at her face it was white and in a scream. The jaws are locked open."

Kyla steps away and I see her find a bin to be sick into. "Okay, O'Halloran, bit more subtle please. She's a little off colour."

"Probably not slept like us all. We found a mass of shredded paper by the machine over there. I presume you want me to try and put them back together?" I nod. "Okay, if I get anything I'll let you know."

"Thanks O'Halloran."

As he goes back to his work, Kyla returns looking a little better. "Don't take this the wrong way, gorgeous," I say, "but you look like shit."

"Thanks!"

"Why don't you go home in a squad car, get some sleep?"

"And you?"

"I'll keep going, get some ideas out of the troops."

Kyla shakes her head. "I'm good."

"Bollocks. You're wrecked."

"I said no." She gives me a look like thunder.

"I insist."

"Piss off," she says, "I said I was okay." She walks off in a huff. I decide to make sure she rests and follow her out of the main office suite towards the elevator outside. She's standing there, as if catching some air. Pressing the door open button, I grab her arm when the doors come apart and drag her inside.

"I said piss off, Mulgrew."

"And you need rest. You're exhausted. Go home, get some sleep."

"Why? Way are you doing this to me?" She's battering me with her fists, thumping my chest, her eyes suddenly erupting into a flood of tears.

"Doing what? I just want you to get some sleep."

She's crying now in fits and starts, still pushing at me. "Just piss off. Bloody man, what do you know?"

I don't understand what I've done. Is it that time of the month? I didn't notice and she's never like this. Trapped together in the elevator, she keeps looking up at me, disappointment in her eyes.

"What, Kyla? What?"

Her voice comes back low and bitter. "You want me to go home, go get some sleep. But I can't. He's over me, I feel him. Do you understand? I'll lie there and he'll be roaming me, feeling me, he'll be…, shit Mulgrew, I want him off me!"

I rush to hold her and she breaks down again in my arms.

"When I go to sleep Mulgrew, I want you there. I want you over me. I want to feel your hands on me. Because just maybe, you'll push him away from me. Just maybe I won't end up like that girl in the tattoo parlour!"

Lifting her face I kiss her. I give her my hands and look her in the eye. Placing them under her top, I find a place I have longed for and I watch her begin to smile. "Don't do anything else, just leave them there. It's better Mulgrew, it's better."

All I can think of is how broke this woman is. And I don't know how to make it go away...., yet.

Chapter 25

It's after midday the next afternoon and we're at a bit of a loss, if we're honest. I have grabbed some downtime by falling into the hammock at the station. As I was dosing off, I felt Kyla arrive but my eyes stayed shut. I think she was standing as she took my hands and that's about all I remember. That's how dog tired I am. But now Hughes has entered the room. And she's talking very fast. Too fast for me.

"Easy Hughes, easy. Say it again, I'm trying to get the engine warmed up again here."

"There's been an abduction, a school. They've abducted a school!"

Now I'm awake and dropping out of my hammock. No way, this is the nightmare. I knew they wanted innocent blood and they had taken homeless and waifs and strays, but it didn't hit home like this. Maybe it should, but it didn't. My stomach is feeling very hollow.

"How long ago?"

"Thirty minutes, Trimble."

"Okay then, Hughes, get me a stack of uniform down there asking questions. Did anyone see anything? What did the kidnappers look like?"

She straightens up as if trying to fortify herself somehow.

"Monk's habits. One described as red haired, seemed to be the leader. And some sort of creature with them."

"Creature?"

"Yes. A hand of knives, one witness said."

I nod, like this is just a normal job we're running. But I need to keep the discipline, go through the normal processes or my mind will just erupt. What else?

"How did they move them?"

"Yellow school bus," says Hughes, "several of them."

"Ok, I'll take Kyla to the scene, Hughes. Where's Gonzales?"

"At home, was due back after dinner."

"Ring him, send him my way. Get Jenny or O'Halloran down to the school with their team. You take the command centre and dial up any CCTV. Pull a couple of uniforms to start checking it all. Licence plates of the buses?"

"Working on it, nothing concrete yet."

"Okay."

I grab my overcoat, shout at Kyla who I see in the offices, and run downstairs meeting Kyla in the car park at the base of the building. The car is waiting for me, door open and she is gripping the wheel tightly as I get in. Without a word she drives out of the car park but her hands are trembling. They are in good company because mine are too.

I need a break, dear God, we need a break. But I also need to think.

"Kyla, how do they do it?"

"A mass execution?"

"Yes, a mass execution. Think about it. They took them in school buses so we will find those soon enough. So they want to be quick. They need to mass execute and then collect the blood. That's the point. They need to collect the blood for the chalice so that others will drink it. Don't look at this as a horror, as a hell, but as a manufacturing problem."

"Seriously, Mulgrew."

"I know that sounds sick but that's what they will be looking at."

"Dear God, it's inhuman."

"Very but how do they do it? If we can work out the how we might just get there before it's too late. They won't want to try and control a large group of kids for too long."

The car goes quiet. I need more details. Taking my cell, I ring Hughes.

"How many kids?"

"Eight hundred!"

"What? How did they just walk out with eight hundred?"

"The creature kept things quiet, we think. But there's a convoy of like twenty school buses. I can't find anything on the CCTV. It's like they just don't exist."

"Keep looking. It may be some sort of trick but keep looking. And Hughes, get someone drawing up locations of all slaughterhouses in the city. Especially the inactive ones, or those only used infrequently. If they are going to kill these kids and collect blood, it'll need some sort of order to it."

"Will do, Trimble. I have SWAT teams ready once we have a location."

"Good. We're here. Will call back very soon."

The scene at the school is a mess. There are reporters crowding around a cordon of uniforms, some of whom are trying to canvas people. I seek out the senior officer and spot Sergeant Hussain. He's a tall man of Middle Eastern origin and I can see he's having trouble holding it all together.

"Hussain, what do we know?"

"Trimble. This shit is like a story from a fairy tale. Apparently this creature enters the school along with a red haired woman dressed as a monk. They stroll right into the assembly hall where the entire school is. Teachers are saying the creature was like hypnotic as they struggled to move. Kids just got up and filed out when the redhead told them to, right onto a mass of yellow buses."

"That's it?"

"He nods his head, looking somewhat glum. "That's all we got. The creature had blades for fingers on one hand. But all descriptions are rather hazy. The redhead had a monk's habit but it was open at the top and the bottom. She was showing a lot of leg and chest. The head teacher, a Mr Houghton, was sexually assaulted as he put it. Sounds like she basically wrapped herself around him and played with his family jewels while she watched the whole thing happen. Got very excited by it all as well. The woman I mean, not the head teacher."

I was hoping for more. Everything was about the drama. No detail about the escape. No licence plates, no directions. Turning to Kyla, I have an apologetic look, because she won't like this task.

"Kyla, get hold of a slaughter house. We need to know how we kill eight hundred children." She looks at me as if I'm crazy. "No, we need to. I need to understand how long it would take to kill and drain the blood, like we do with animals. Dammit Kyla, I know it's sick and I can't believe I'm saying it, but I need to understand what sort of facility and how quickly they can do it."

She nods and swears but the curse is drowned out by a helicopter overhead. It's a television company. Sick buggers. Pulling out my cell phone, I contact Hughes again. "Get a squad car down to every slaughterhouse in the city. Used and disused. If we know it exists then check it." I can hear the tremble in her voice as she speaks back. I guess this hits parents even harder. I look at the cordon behind me and there's a multitude of crying parents and more coming all the time.

And right now I have nothing for them. Just nothing.

Chapter 26

My brain is scrambled. I'm gambling that my thought process is right on this one, looking at the practical issues as opposed to the emotional ones, to work out where the kids are. A uniform's been interviewing the head teacher, trying to see if he knows anything. Apparently the redhead taunted him, played about with him.

And then it strikes me. We need to know more about her. Maybe there's detail in her background. She might seem a demon but she's very human and she'll have a background. Maybe that influences her decisions. 'Cos she seems to be the main leader, outside of the demon itself.

And it's a crazy hunch that's forming in my head but it might just be something. Records, I need records. I interrupt the uniform talking to the head teacher.

"What did she call you? What name did she use with you?" He's a bit put out that I have just barged in but that's tough. "Think, man. What did she call you?"

The man is a quivering wreck. "Sir, she said, Sir. I told her we don't use that anymore but she still kept on saying it."

"Are there any photographs? Anywhere with visual records?"

"Well yes, there's a whole line of school photographs, year on year in the main corridor to the staff room. It's only accessible to the teachers."

"Take me, take me there now," I say, calling over Kyla from a distance away. She's going to have to wait for an explanation. The man stumbles as he leads the way. I'd like to be easier on him but there's no time. I need to think this through.

"Kyla, our redhead friend, how old? How old would you say?"

"Hard to say. Early thirties at best, maybe younger."

I reckon she's right which makes it late nineties to the early part of this century that she'd feature as a child. We enter a hallway of photographs, large wide panoramic shots of an entire school. I start at a year marked 1995. There's a sea of faces, nothing outstanding, no red head. Onto 1996, and I spend a good minute looking.

"What is it, Mulgrew?"

"Something in what she did to the head teacher. Just a hunch."

1997 and I see a small red head girl sitting beside a male teacher. She's just a child but I recognise the eyes. "Kyla, look here." I point at the girl.

"No way! That's her."

But I'm onto 1998. She's there again. And right beside the same man. And 1999. And 2000. I grab the head teacher. "Who's that man?"

"That's Mr Culder, he was the head teacher two people before me."

"Do you have an address?"

"Yes, probably."

"Quickly, I need it, his life might be in danger."

The man scurries off and Kyla looks at me quizzically.

"Danger. I thought it was the kids that were in danger."

"Oh they are. But I think she came back to torment an abuser. Either that or he may be gone already. Just a hunch. We may get a name for her too."

There's a nervous wait as we check the photographs time and again, looking at the young face of the woman that has caused so much death and destruction. But in the photos she looks innocent of anything. Sullen and moody but not the wild creature she is today. Everyone's got a story, that's what my Mom used to say, everyone. And she's right.

The head teacher comes running back along the corridor towards me holding a slip of paper in his hand. "This is it. The last address we have for him. He was back here two years ago during a celebration for our high achieving pupils."

I grab the piece of paper and ask the man to follow me. Kyla's on my heels, but I'm looking for Hussain. When I can't see him immediately I head for a nearby Sergeant running the scene, handing him the paper and saying, "Uniforms, this address now. Don't enter unless you suspect a life is in trouble."

I've got the wheel as we head the short distance to the address. Kyla's watching me the whole time. Without looking I can feel her eyes on me, questioning, wondering about me. Then it arrives.

"Are you okay, Mulgrew?"

"Hardly. I've just realised that this bitch from hell may have been created by someone. I was running the premise she was just gaga and did this to herself. The last thing I want to feel about her is pity."

"It's normal to feel pity for her, despite all she's done, easier to write it off."

"But the stuff that's happening. She's got children and

intends to kill them. Kyla, I can't feel pity for her. I shouldn't."

She lets it go and we arrive quickly at the address. There are two squad cars there and I nod at the officers I find. "Hold the perimeter whilst Corstain and I go in. We'll holler if something's up."

The house seems silent. I push the front door and find it open, on the latch. It's a smart place, a lot of the recent gadgets, a pretty sharp look to the decor. There are photographs showing a man with a woman, both in their later years. More photographs adorn the hallway, again of the pair. I can't see any children in any of the photographs, so it looks like they are a childless couple.

Turning left, I enter a living room and see a computer on a large coffee table. There are printouts around the computer and my eyes recoil at the images. There's no blood, no gore, just acts suited to the adult realm. But not all the actors are adults. I move away from the images as quick as I can until a face grabs my attention. A red head, and the eyes I know, sullen and empty.

"Mulgrew!"

I follow the sound of Kyla's voice to the next room. A naked man lies propped up on the floor. There's a pool of blood from between his legs. Probably easiest to say there's a gap where other things should be. As a cop, I have developed an unemotional response to seeing gruesome images, a cold distance mainly. But I find myself thinking this bastard got what he deserved. Maybe he did, but that's not how a cop should think.

Chapter 27

" I get the feeling this was personal."

Kyla looks at me as if I've gone mad. "Of course it was personal, look at the things he did to her. It was very personal. Part of me doesn't blame her for doing this to him."

"I mean it's out of character. A cry for pity. That man is no innocent. She could have killed him anytime over this last year or so, or even before. But she did it now. And then there's the school. Why that one? It just happens to be her old school."

"Well, she got vengeance."

"When has that been a motive? In all our dealings we have never been looking at vengeance. Not from her. She may have used vengeance sought by others to her ends, like with this chalice. But she's a servant and she, up until now, has been following the master plan. There's something wrong, something I can't place my finger on."

Kyla looks sceptical, her eyebrows raised. "Meanwhile we have hundreds of children about to be executed. I'd say not that much has changed."

She has a point. During all my efforts to see a chink, a way into this redhead's mind, I have to be careful not to forget those still in danger. Pulling out my cell I ring Hughes for an update. It seems no one knows anything, a cavalcade of yellow school buses has just vanished. No CCTV, nothing. It isn't normal, rather there's something behind it, masking it. People would have noticed them.

"Hughes, have we looked around the local area? The area around the school. Any abattoirs?"

"There are a few, Trimble, but we had uniform all over them and there's nothing."

I sit on the bonnet of the car and think through what's happening. Surely my methodology is correct. They need somewhere large and with collection points for the blood. Abattoirs would do that. Poultry processing too but that's part of Hughes' list. But the whole thing this time has been personal. Completely personal. So maybe the place they are going to is personal.

"Kyla, we need to look at those photographs in the house. See if we can identify a common place, somewhere that's reused a lot."

"Why? What's that to do with the missing kids?"

"This has all been personal. All been about her. Maybe a purging of her past. I don't know but it all seems strange."

"Okay, let's look." She's not impressed with the idea and I don't blame her. These may be the last images on earth I want to look at.

Knelt before the table in the living room, Kyla starts going through each picture before passing it to me. We work quick, looking beyond the people to the background and the places. I have no idea how the teams that cover this sort of work manage it. I would give up being a cop.

As Kyla hands me the photographs, I also separate any containing our red head. She seems to be in about a quarter of the pictures, always with Mr Culder. And always inside, many in the same room. But there's also one outstanding picture that is outside. Our redhead is fully clothed, as is Mr Culder, in a park of some sort.

"Kyla, this one."

"Yeah, thought that was weird. Looks more like a family picture than this filth he's got."

"Yes, but where is that?" I get to my feet and go outside to one of the local uniforms. I wave the picture in front of his face. The thick set, black man takes it from me and studies it.

"Where is that Officer?"

He shakes his head. "I'm not sure, could be a number of places, we have quite a few parks around here. Unless…?"

"What? Unless what?" I demand.

"Just a second. Flaherty, come here a moment." He waves to his colleague and a balding white haired officer comes over. "Look at that. Is that the old park?"

"Yes," says Flaherty, "Got concreted over about five years back. There's no grass there anymore."

I feel deflated. I was so sure this would be something. "So it's totally gone. Nothing left?"

The black officer nods. "The only thing left was the old telephone exchange on the edge of the place. The land there was owned by a conglomerate of some sort and they decided to hang on to it as the value has been rising steadily."

"How big's that building?"

"Oh, massive," says Flaherty, "but full of that old style telephone exchanges, you know rows and rows of them, all super redundant now."

"But could you fit eight hundred kids in there?"

The officers look up at me, quizzically. "Well you could, I guess. There are a few rooms out the back but they couldn't hold all the kids. But if you used up the exchange parts, all the long corridors and other floor space. Yeah, you could do it fairly easily."

"Get in the car, Flaherty. And you, what's your name Officer."

"Adebayo, sir."

"Get in with Flaherty and wait for me to follow you. Get me to this telephone exchange. Make sure you come out armed."

I run inside and call Kyla to follow me. As I sink into the driver's seat, I tell her to call for back-up and ask HQ to get a location on our car tracker. This is a hunch but I hope it's a good one.

Chapter 28

The blood is pumping through my veins as our vehicle races behind the squad car in front of us. My hands are clammy, the sweat making them sticky and I feel a little helpless as Kyla drives. I can feel her tension as well, as she doesn't speak, merely focusing instead on the road ahead.

The telephone exchange is not far away and as the car in front pulls up, I check my weapon before stepping out of my own transport. Kyla is flanking me almost instantly and I ask the officers to lead us to the easiest access.

Running across open ground to the main entrance of the building, a grey and formidable structure before us with only a few windows, I hear a shot ring out and run for cover. Once established behind a concrete bollard, I look over my shoulder to find Kyla looking at me intently, hidden from anyone in the building by a recess. The officers have scattered the other way and I'm only presuming from the lack of shouts that they are okay.

The shot came from high up and the building must have at least six or seven floors. It could be a rabbit warren in there and I don't like the thought of trying to close quarter fight, surrounded by a large number of schoolkids ready to become collateral damage. On the other hand, I don't want to wait for back up as they may have already started on the butchering.

Kyla gives me a nod indicating she is going to come round behind me and make an approach to the building's front doors. They are made of wood with reinforced glass allowing a view into the exchange but there are no lights beyond. It's a risky ploy and I don't know if my covering fire will be enough but we need to get inside.

She sets off, and I refrain from watching her magnificent form in full flight and instead roll up from behind my cover and fire off shots towards the top of the building. I think I can see someone there but these are really just warning blows, hopefully keeping any would-be shooter behind their cover. The uniforms must be okay as I hear them giving further cover.

As Kyla approaches the door, I begin to run and I see her firing though the glass. There's a shatter but the door is still reasonably intact, holes instead appearing through the reinforced medium. As Kyla reaches the door, I see her open it easily and step inside. Although I feel out of breath already, I drive my legs to get inside to help her. In the distance I can hear sirens and help arriving.

Opening the door, I see Kyla on her knee inside covering a passageway. She doesn't even glance at me and I run ahead to the opening, juking my head inside briefly. It's dark and I cannot see anything ahead but I wonder if that's simply because my eyes have not adjusted to the dark. I run up the corridor and hear Kyla get up behind me. The corridor is tight, maybe enough for two persons but it soon splits into a small room.

I barely see the blade coming towards me but I crumple to a heap as it comes at my left side. A blur of thin metal passes above my head and I slide on into the room. I presume my attacker looked to come after me because I hear a shot ring out from the corridor and there's a thud behind me as I try to scrabble to my feet.

There's a monk's habit on the floor, occupied by a man with a sword. Kyla, her shooting always much more accurate than mine, seems to have shot him in the head. I look around the room, checking for other intruders. A yell breaks from a doorway beyond me and another monk figure runs at me with a machete raised. I think about discharging my weapon but instinct takes over and I merely step aside and catch my attacker with a simple trip.

The figure goes down hard and slides into the wall. Before she can move, and it is a she as the now exposed legs are pale and slender, never a man's legs, I am on top removing the machete from her grasp. The woman tries to roll over and a hand reaches out searching for my face. I plant a severe right hand into her jaw and she drops. It's only then that I see that the attacker is just a kid, maybe sixteen or seventeen.

"The uniforms are right behind us," informs Kyla as she enters from the corridor. Looking down at me she sees my attacker. "That's a kid, Mulgrew."

I roll the girl over and her habit reveals more of her figure and I find myself pulling back. There's not much clothing underneath, in fact she reminds me of a redhead I know, one with eyes of hate.

"Come on, Mulgrew, the uniforms are coming, let's keep going."

I nod at Kyla and she looks at the doorway my attacker came through. "I'll stay on lead Kyla," I say, "You have the better covering shot." There's no argument and I head through the door carefully.

The door opens to a staircase and two doors. I'm wondering

how to play this when Flaherty arrives and I can see more men behind him. "Flaherty, secure this point as an exit. Then as numbers arrive flood the lower level first, before sending teams up the stairs. There was a shooter above when we approached and who knows how many they have here. But these guys don't hang about so don't wait too long." I turn to Kyla. "We'll start up the stairs."

Quickly, we sweep up the stairs and find a door two flights up and more stairs continuing upwards. I tell Kyla to watch the stairs above and I open the door. Inside is dark but I can feel a presence. Beyond me are tall racks of old telephone exchanges and they are arranged to give a space between each, making artificial corridors.

As my eyes adjust to the near dark, I can see kids sitting in the space between each line of exchanges, all with their hands on their heads. I step inside the door and let it close quietly behind me. There's a roaming monk up ahead but he hasn't turned my way, so I hunch down.

I think the figure up ahead is a man but the image of the girl I knocked out down below comes to mind. Then I see the young acolyte holding the knife over me at the wildlife park. There's a rage building inside me and I fight to keep it in check. I need to be cool and calm.

I start to shuffle forward slowly towards the figure ahead, my weapon trained on him lest he turn and look at me. But he's engaged in something, and I see a schoolgirl being made to stand. There's another monk with him that I can see beyond the exchanges. One runs a hand across the girl's behind before making her sit down roughly. Then another girl is made to stand and again a hand runs across her rear. The dirty Johns.

There's the slightest sound, almost inconsequential, but the door behind me has opened and closed. It's probably Kyla but I don't look round. Instead, I keep moving forward. I become aware that the line of exchanges to my left have gaps through them and there are kids sat on the other side from me. Who knows how many kids are there? Who knows how many attackers in this particular room, which appears to be the size of a small soccer pitch?

So far I have surprise, so far all is quiet. But then I see a hand from the corner of my eye reaching out of the space between the exchanges. It taps my shoulder and is pale and white. I turn briefly to give acknowledgement but the eyes I see are wide open on a face that is wholly terrified. The girl can only be maybe thirteen but she is trembling. I hold up a hand and she seems to be partially placated until her eyes see my weapon ahead of me. She shakes and I know what's coming. Dear God, no! She can't!

The girl lets out an almighty scream.

Chapter 29

One of the monks comes towards the sound and on seeing me pulls a knife from inside his habit. There's a hand reaching for the nearest kid and I don't hesitate, letting a volley go into the monk who is flung backwards by the shot, landing in a heap on the floor. I don't stop but rise instead to my feet, seeking out the other monk who has grabbed one of the school girls.

I don't trust a shot at this distance with a hostage covering most of my target and I run round the exchanges to confront the dark clad man. The time it takes me to round the corner is too long and he should have stabbed his victim but she shows remarkable courage driving her elbows into him. It's not a blow that wounds him but it is enough to throw him off balance for a moment. As he grabs her hair, pulling her back into the shape he wants her, I am able to barrel into him, taking the three of us to the ground.

It's a reckless dive and I go down hard, my shoulder landing awkwardly, my gun slipping from my grasp. But before I can stand I hear shots ringing out, driving away the screams of the children, and the monk who has risen quickly falls again.

"Mulgrew, you okay?" shouts Kyla.

I feel like my shoulder's been removed and put back again

but I need to be okay. Beside me the girl who was in the monk's grasp is on her knees screaming. I get to my own knees and try to throw a comforting arm around her but Kyla pushes me off.

"Like she needs a man she doesn't know after what they were doing," tuts Kyla.

She's probably right but I was only trying to be of comfort. There's more to do and I ditch my wounded pride and start telling the kids to go back the way I came in. As I take the other exit from the room I see officers start to enter from the rear door.

The rest of the floor is full of kids, all sat in huddles too scared to move. Quickly, we work our way up the floors until there is only the roof left. A small band of monks has gathered there and they have a hostage with them. I get to the door that leads out to the roof and see a huddle of habits. I am informed that there is a girl inside that ring. So far the officers haven't moved on it as she appears to be alright. By that I guess they mean intact.

From our standpoint the struggle to regain the building and the kids has gone well and we have control of everything except the roof. But as I breathe hard, grabbing my breath back and watching this ring of monks from the door, I cannot help but think something is wrong. Since when have they taken hostages? In the other rooms they moved to kill when discovered and yet here they are looking to do what? Book a passage out of here? I step out onto the roof.

"Don't come closer," shouts a monk at the front, brandishing a knife. "Or we will cut her. She'll be sliced and diced before you can get to us."

The voice is not confident and I would normally think that

appropriate but these are not ordinary criminals or thugs. The monks usually do not engage in conversation. The only one who has is the redhead.

"Stay back Trimble, or we will kill her."

Trimble? How do they know my name? She does. But no foot soldier has ever called me that. I hear moans from inside the ring of monks and continue to walk slowly forward. I hear Kyla walking behind me, probably anxious that I am walking away from my back-up.

"Trimble?" I say. "Detective Trimble to you."

From inside the ring there are more groans and moans, like you would hear in an alleyway on a Saturday night, two heavy handed lovers enjoying themselves. No, this is not right.

"Open up and let me see your victim," I shout. "I don't believe you have anyone in there."

The monk who spoke is rattled and I can see his face telling me he needs instructions. He wants to turn and ask someone, someone who is in the middle of the ring but he also doesn't want to give his cards away.

"Let me see who you have!" I yell.

There is some sort of command I can't hear because the monks split. In the middle with her back to me is a woman wearing a white school blouse with a skirt having fallen to the ground. Her buttocks are bare and shapely and I swear she is almost displaying them at me, tempting me with them. But I see the red hair and I know who this is.

"Trimble, you came for me. You saw what that headmaster did to me, and you came to save me. My hero, Kyle."

I hear Kyla spit into the ground as the red head mentions my name, my first name. Only my mother, God rest her soul, got to call me that. I draw my weapon but the redhead remains with her back to me.

"Now, now. There's no need for that, Kyle. Lovers shouldn't argue. Doesn't the schoolgirl look work for you? I bet she wouldn't dress up like this for you."

Despite the grotesque nature of what she is doing, I struggle to think straight. It's like an enchantment, a compulsion to watch. She undoes her shirt and drops it leaving her totally bare with her back to me.

"Poor Kyle, you will so beat yourself up over this. Remember if you need to take out your frustrations you can always take them out on me. I'll do everything she won't for you. You know I will. Give you a position to rule as well. Get you over the pain and anger you are about to feel."

"What pain and anger?" shouts Kyla. "What the hell are you on about?"

"The bitch speaks. You won't console him from this."

The skies suddenly darken and from nowhere it begins to rain. With an unnatural pace, the rain intensifies and there is lightening and the heavy growl of thunder in a rapid succession.

"The school kids, I knew they would draw you, I knew. And they are all safe. You have saved them. Well done, Kyle." She lets go a wild cackle, a laugh full of hate and vile before turning around and showing her full bare self. I want to look away but I can't. It's not just her image, because the one thing I cannot pull away from is her eyes.

"Take them home to their grateful parents, Kyle. Receive the thanks, the prayers of those good people. And then wallow in the guilt because you screwed up. You got it wrong. She won't be able to lift the guilt from you, Kyle. Because I have the blood. Lots of it, dripping red and innocent. You think you have seen hell? Now we come, Kyle. And your blind bitch won't stop him. And I'll have you as we kill your woman on an altar to the fallen one."

There's a gunshot and the redhead's shoulder is tagged. I flinch from my trance as more shots are fired. But none hit the redhead who is engulfed by the monks. As a band they encircle her, ignoring any fellow monks who fall from Kyla's shots. They walk slowly toward the roof edge. I can do nothing but stand and stare as they simply fall off the edge. As the last topples, I manage to break free from the bind and race to the edge.

Seven floors down is a mess of monk's habits and shattered bodies. But there is no redhead, no naked woman. And the words ring in my head. *I have the blood. Dripping and red and innocent.* I shiver and my stomach churns. And then from behind me I hear an officer say "Sir, sir. You need to come."

Chapter 30

The new Chief has always seemed to be as tough emotionally as anyone. He's been helpful, driven and practical in these weird days but today he is most definitely human. I'm standing with him at the homeless shelter where a couple of hours ago they were serving lunch to the many that walk through their door. And I mean many. Usually it's three to four hundred that pass through.

Today there's at least three hundred and twenty-five. That's the number of bodies we have separated and counted. We're trying to be professional, trying to get on with the job. I see Jenny Tatler and O'Halloran holding back all emotion as they guide their scene of crime teams. But Jenny is shaking at times and O'Halloran is incredibly silent and not complaining about anything.

The Chief was in here for five minutes before he said he needed to get some air. I found him alone, behind a garbage can crying his eyes out. I joined him. There are some things in this life you should never see let alone have to work through. Today was one of them.

Now we look on in silence each pondering where we go from here. The large dining room is a bloody maelstrom of our homeless from this area. A tribute to evil, to sickness, to wild and mad things. Very few people have seen this and that's how it is going to stay. Jenny and O'Halloran will gather all the evidence, sort out the bodies and then place them somewhere sterile but at rest. A place where relatives, if they have any, can gather, a place where the city can grieve. Here is not that place.

I turn and walk outside for some air. We are keeping everyone at least a block away so there's no cameras in my face as we exit. I see Kyla talking to Hughes and her face is all concern as she spots me.

"Mulgrew," she says as she approaches, "Don't!"

"She said it. I would feel guilty, I would feel it. And I bloody do. I bought it, hook, line and sinker. I followed her like a puppet on a string, convinced of my cleverness. Rushed like a hero. I am such a dumb ass."

"It's not your fault. You didn't do this."

"But I should have stopped it." I spit on the ground. "This is too much. This is too far." There's tears in my eyes. "Dammit Kyla, those poor bastards never stood a chance."

I can feel her hold me but I'm numb. There's a strange silence for a crime scene. Around the hustle and bustle of so many people moving, all conversations are hushed. Normally the area would be a cacophony of noise but today it is almost quiet. No dark jokes like we usually have, no conversations outside of the work. I'm sure many are thinking of their families and those who have to face this.

A car pulls up in front of the building. It's a green dodge and a thin, frail nun steps out. She has no eyes and yet was in the driver's seat. Normally the arrival of Sister Martha is a good thing but today I feel like a failure.

"Why are you here, Detective?

"I still have a job to do," I say, breaking off from Kyla. "We have a horde of people to identify. Traces to find so we can get the bastards who did this. That's why I'm here. Despite screwing this up I am here."

"Stop it! Just stop it!" says the nun.

"Don't start today, not today of all days!"

"We have work to do, Detective."

"What work? They did it, they got the blood." I hang my head in shame. "She tricked me and they got it."

"Yes they did."

"Is that it, all you have to say?" I wish she would just go. It's like being caught by your mom.

"And what of you, Detective Corstain? Will you wallow here too?" asks Sister Martha.

"Wallow? Don't you get it, we messed up, and they are dead," retorts Kyla.

"That is so. But I let this demon through so I hold the blood on my hands too. But see past yourselves for this is a mere trifle. What is to come will be a hundredfold what you have seen if it is not stopped."

"Trifle?" says Kyla, "How can you call this a trifle?"

"You have seen nothing, nothing at all. Go home. Shower or at least clean up. Reconcile the things between you. And then meet me on the beach, beyond the city, the place where you first tangled with the redheaded one. But be reconciled."

"Reconciled?" asks Kyla.

"Yes, reconciled. His guilt of looking at her. Your guilt of not allowing him to touch you. His anger at the demon that has come between. Your frustrations that he feels he is too old for you. I was once a partner, a lover, a special one. Reconcile or you won't survive the next trial."

"What do you mean, reconcile?" I ask, still brooding from this scolding.

"Man and woman, reconcile and be united. Otherwise they will break you apart. The next time they will unleash their horde, in numbers you have not seen so far. We need to stop it, find and kill the head. But you will see things that you cannot handle if there are doubts and fears between you. Reconcile."

I look at Kyla who at least seems to understand what Martha is saying.

"And then the beach. Quickly."

Kyla takes my hand. And there's a faint smile as she looks at me. "Come on, you tell the Chief."

Chapter 31

When I told the Chief that we needed to go, I didn't exactly tell him the whole truth. All I said was that there was something new that had come from Sister Martha, something that needed to be looked at right away. This was because I really was not sure what I was going away to. But there was something about Kyla, something that was changing from despair into something positive.

When we got back to my place, she told me to go and get a shower. I was pretty insistent that we needed to hurry and get to the beach with Sister Martha but she got hold of me. Not in a shouting match but with a tender hand that took my own and just gently held it, running her fingers across the back of mine.

Stood in the shower, I let the water just flow over my head but the guilt of seeing the dead at the homeless shelter grabbed me again. My shoulders shook as I cried. It was the blood and mess that hit me when I first stood looking at the site. And then I felt her laughing, the redheaded one, her face above me, mocking me. Worse still her body, her flesh crying out to me. Like a cheap plastic toy won in a fair, I knew she would simply play with me before throwing me away, a mere curiosity to be won and then abandoned.

I didn't even hear Kyla step into the shower. First a kiss between my shoulder blades which made me start to turn around but her arms wrapped me up from behind. They searched me in a determined fashion and I could feel her stand on her tip toes, pulling herself close to rest a chin on my shoulder. Like a blanket she enfolded me, and sent a shiver across me as our skin touched. She would not let me do anything but be held as she whispered in my ear, barely audible above the sound of falling water.

"This is our place, she's not allowed in here. And he isn't on me. This is where I own you and you own me. Tell me, what you fear, tell me what you don't want to say about her to me. Whenever she entices, let me be there to send that vile bitch away. Let me fight for you."

And I stood for what seemed like an eternity. How could I tell her about how my body was gripped at times by this devil? How I had immediately sought a redemption for her, to excuse what she was, to find her and save her? Not because of some noble cause but because she was really under my skin. She was slowly dragging me in and then mocking me. Mocking me by having me charge to her and miss the deaths of all those poor lost people.

And then hands grabbed me and Kyla cried out that this was hers to own, this was all her own. Her hands raked my chest and her lips kissed my neck and she held me like someone possessed. But this was a different possession. One of hunger and passion, yes, but one of a love that wanted me to be me, to stand with me and hold me up.

And then she told me what he was doing to her, the every moment horror of how she felt him invading her, of touching her although he was nowhere to be seen. Feeling scared of her vulnerability, I just stood there, letting her vent her frustration, her anger until she became suddenly silent.

I was unsure of what she wanted, of what I could do. Having been on an emotional high of her grabbing me and holding me through my pain, I was unsure if I simply should hold her. And then the moment seemed to slide away like we had just taken a wrong turn and slid off the road, our car free falling off the cliff edge with only the rocks below to await us. Disaster awaited.

Sometimes in life, I simply react without knowing what the other person or situation really requires. Where your head would say, don't do anything, just wait and see, I strike out on my path. Maybe it's instinct, or maybe the depths of my brain understanding something I cannot put my finger on.

Kyla had turned and had pushed open the door of the shower when I turned around and grabbed her hand. I whispered that she was mine, and then I had no words. Was it passion, was it hunger? Was it a daft old fool making his desperate bid for something tumbling from his grasp? I don't know. But as I took her in my arms, she cried. At first I went to break off but she hauled my arms in close and intimate.

Now in the car as she drives, I look across at her. The hair is tied up in her ponytail and I watch her neck. She knows I'm looking and smiles. As the car swerves through the traffic, I think of how in those early days I simply wanted to have her as my own. But now I see that as the early stages, and maybe it was more physical. Don't get me wrong, this is still physical but it's a whole lot more than that.

What strikes me is that despite standing under that shower facing each other and seeing my dream before me, it's not her image that keeps coming to mind. Right here and now, as I look at her simply driving, it's her words that replay to me, like a mantra girding me for what is to come. Words that say more than any touch or act can do.

"I own you, and you own me. Every damn bit, Mulgrew, every damn piece of me."

Chapter 32

As Kyla parks the car at the edge of the beach, I see Sister Martha, back to us, staring out at the sea. When I first saw her, Martha was not exactly spritely but she held herself with a dignity. Now she looks weary, her shoulders slumping and her hips misaligned, one slightly higher than the other in what would seem an uncomfortable stance.

"Why here?" Kyla asks me as we exit the car but I just shrug. This is where I escaped to while following the redhead after we infiltrated the Sanderson building, the destination of the portal I had to choose when all others were seemingly closed. And after capturing her with the help of a colleague, she vanished from underneath her habit.

Stepping across the sand, I feel a chill. Before Kyla arrived I had a healthy skepticism about the spiritual world, one that believed in miracles and bad guys and angels. But not like this. Sometimes I think my sanity will just get up and walk.

"You are prepared, Detective?" says Sister Martha as we approach.

"I'm armed as ever and I think I am ready,"

"We are ready," says Kyla, flashing a knowing look at the nun who simply smiles. I get the feeling, like men often do, that women speak another language and we're not even close to the party.

"But why are we here?" I ask.

"Detective, so far we have been reacting to everything they have done. We have, or rather you have tried to follow leads and get ahead of them. You did that with some, other situations you dealt with as best you could.

"But now we enter a different phase. No longer can we simply hope to track them down, try to retake the cup before it does such damage. Now we need to destroy this demon, turn its physical body to dust and send the creature back to the abyss. We must enter its lair and hunt it down, go past its minions and monsters, whatever form they take."

"But why here?" I reiterate.

"Because here, Detective, I can find a way in. There has been a portal here created by their sorcery, as you may call it. I can find the taint and from that I can find its stronghold." The nun shifts uneasily as she says the words.

"So why not do that before?" asks Kyla.

"Because my dear, it hadn't decided to unleash its horde. Now it has the blood it will sit in its stronghold and unleash wave after wave upon this city and then the country and then the earth. Until now it did not see fit to show its hand but rather it slunk in the shadows. Now it will not hide but send forth.

"As we speak, they will be drinking the blood and be sent out. It will send out those filled with rage and hate and your armies and police will not hold them forever. They may hold back the tide but the waves that follow will sweep them aside until more are sent. Only with the defeat of the demon will the curse lift and order be restored. You have the knife?"

"Yes," I say, "of course."

The nun turns and looks at me in that curious way she has, the head pointing at me but no eyes being present. "We will need help, just a few and strong. Those who have seen the madness. There will be physical beings we can defeat with might, guns if you wish and so we should bring friends who can fight. But they need to be strong in mind and in spirit for there will be much that cannot be fought with that of the physical realm.

"I am going to track down the demon's lair. It may take an hour, it may take several, but you should gather our forces, Detective. Good people, ones you can rely on. I have already sent for spiritual reinforcements, they will be here presently. Now leave me be and go to your work."

I look at Kyla and she indicates we should go back to the car. I watch Martha sit down on the sand and raise her arms up high. She begins to hum and I watch her body shake.

"I thought I was clear, Detective, you have your job, I have mine. Let's get about our business."

"Sorry," I say, "we'll get on."

Kyla's ahead of me and she is a sight for these troubled times. It's easy to lose myself in her until the thought strikes of where the Sister said we would go. It's the last place I would want Kyla. Last time she lost the use of her legs. What will be the cost this time?

"Don't worry," she says reading my mind. "This is a calling, this is a higher purpose. Remember, you own me and I own you. We can't lose each other."

I wish it seemed that simple to me but I turn my attention to who we should bring along with us. Hughes, Kobold and Gonzales come to mind and that would leave the Chief short of those who know what's going on. But if what the Sister says is right, if we don't succeed then all is lost anyway. So I tell Kyla to call them in and to load up.

Then I remember the situation at the school. The SWAT team that went in have experience of these rage fueled people the blood creates. They would be a good addition. So again I tell Kyla to get organizing. And then comes the inevitable call from the Chief.

"Trimble, do you want every useful person I have? And what do you want them for anyway?"

I wish this was in person so the Chief could see my face because my voice is going to sound all sorts of crazy. But it's too late to go into a lot of detail. And anyway what detail do I have. "Sir, there will be an attack coming out of a central place. An attack of crazies like you have seen before but on a much larger scale. You will need to evacuate everyone and ring fence it off. Evacuate for miles, empty the city if you have to. I don't know how you will convince people of that, but you need to."

I look up at Kyla and she shrugs her shoulders. I had hoped she would have some words I could use to be more convincing but alas, no.

"You need to trust me on this one. We're going to infiltrate this stronghold they will come out of, and take off the snake's head so to speak. Where? I don't know where, but we will. If we don't come back? Well sir, if we don't come back this will be a country-wide problem and then maybe the world. Find people who know about these things from wherever and don't hold back. Yeah, I'd be looking at the military too."

I've just handed him the largest plate of foul smelling crap possible but the man still wishes me good luck and God speed. I know he doesn't fully understand but he's trusting me on this. I guess dealing with the bombs when the demon first arrived has given me a lot of stock.

Hughes rolls up in a station car with Kobold and Gonzales. Reaching into the trunk of the car, she starts equipping herself like it's Armageddon. Well, maybe she's right. A black van pulls up and I watch twelve officers dressed in urban blacks with automatic rifles and a pile of other gear step out. I recognize their leader, Farra.

"Good to have you, Farra. Corstain will brief you but this will be strange. And you'll be taking instruction from that woman out there on the sand."

Farra looks at Sister Martha who is chanting and currently floating about three inches above the sand. "Yes sir, Corstain." His words are perfect but his face shows how he knows he has walked into the madhouse.

Chapter 33

I think about how famous leaders have prepared their soldiers for battle and none come to mind who sent a colleague off to get the coffee while everyone else watched a nun floating in midair. Kobold's return, along with a bucket load of coffee and donuts is welcome but it does little to take off the edge I am feeling. Sister Martha said an hour or two. It's now dark and the midnight hour is at hand. Above us the moon shines brightly, not quite full but looking ominous.

"Do you always surround yourself with such people?" asks Farra.

"When you see where we are going you'll be asking why I didn't take more like her. The answer is I don't know any others like her." I turn and watch Sister Martha with everyone else. She has not had any food nor drink. The weary look she started with has not diminished but she has been persistent. And then with a bump she lands on the sand and collapses. Kyla is the first to her and I follow at my slower pace.

"It is okay, child," she says to Kyla who tries to help her up, "Just give me a moment."

Kyla steps back and soon the Sister is surrounded by the entire team. Farra gently strokes his rifle and displays a face full of questions but he understands authority and so bides his time.

"I have it, Trimble, I have the location."

"Where?" I ask the Sister. "Where is it and I'll get the area cleared?"

"No, you misunderstand how this works. I can take us there. But we will travel through another way, another dimension if you please. I only know the route not the destination until I get there. I will open up a path, a portal even if that's easier to understand, but until I step through I will not know where it is."

"But it will be where the demon is?" I ask.

"Have you not seen me work, Trimble? Do I look like an imbecile? Of course it is where the demon will be, but it will be on the edge of the stronghold. I dare not arrive in too strong a fashion lest they smite us too heavily too quickly. We need to infiltrate, not attack Trimble. You there, the man with the rifle, SWAT team?"

"Yes Ma'am," says Farra, suddenly clocking Sister Martha's lack of eyes which strangely enough seem to be staring intently.

"You understand, infiltrate? Quiet, unseen. The goal is the demon. The goal is to place the knife in the corporeal form of the demon. Anything less and we will lose it all. If you move to protect innocents we find, you will be exposed to the demon and we will struggle to get near it. So we go quietly and with one focus. Everyone, understand. And if you are seen then you step away from us and fight with everything you have to distract it."

Her look is fierce and she scans everyone with it. Only then does she haul herself up off the floor. It seems to be more of an effort than it should and I step forward to help her but she shakes me off.

"This is not about the strength of the body, Detective. If it was, I would be dead weeks ago."

With that she walks slowly away to a distant part of the sand and begins to wave her hands in the air. Before us a circle opens up and it is like looking through a viewer. There is commotion and fire.

"It has begun. Look all of you, this is the stronghold. At present I am only looking from outside. But I shall find a place for us to enter so gird yourselves, weapons and minds at the ready."

I feel Kyla take my hand and in front of everyone she kisses me on the cheek, with no embarrassment and no hesitation. *I own you and you own me*, she mouths. I see Hughes look at me and I hold up a fist. She acknowledges with her own fist and then looks over the rest of the band of insurgents. Hughes has been grounded before by this darkness but many here will have no idea what toll this will take. Maybe they are in the better position.

Sister Martha continues to move her hands and the view in the circle passes by corners of buildings and then disappears into a room. There is little light and the scene is hard to fathom but the Sister seems to be happy as she gives a sigh.

"It will be open for less than thirty seconds so when I say move, everyone move in and stay silent. When inside be prepared for instruction. Do not proceed until instructed. No radios, no telephones."

"Should I not tell the Chief where this is happening?" I ask.

"It is happening and if he does not know already, he will in a matter of minutes."

As if on cue my mobile rings, as does Kyla's and Farra's and many others.

"Drop them with the radios. Leave them all behind. Do not speak. Motion with hands only. They can make you hear things but they won't control your hands."

Soon a pile of advanced communication devices sits on the sand. They are vibrating and buzzing but no one is answering.

"And watch your minds. Discern what you see. Know those that you see. They will use distraction and misrepresentation to disarm you, to sweep you aside. Hear me and follow. Whatever you see, hear me and follow my directions."

With that Sister Martha sweeps her hands in front of the portal and it becomes clearer, like a veil has been dropped. I step through motioning the others to follow. I hear the beach behind me, the waves gently running onto the sand. I taste the salt air on my lips and then see Sister Martha step through and swing her hands closing the opening. And now there is just a stench. It's one I have smelt before. It's death, and death in abundance.

Chapter 34

Although the room in which we arrive is dark, there are noises outside, shouts and cries. It sounds as if a commotion is building, a fermenting and aggressive cry to the world. My hand rests on my weapon and I see Farra tense up. Sister Martha walks through us to the far side of the dark room, but she's merely a shape so poor is the light.

"Remember," she states in a calm voice, "we are not here to save people, we are here to kill a demon. Only that will allow us to achieve our goal, only that will truly save people. Anything you see could be trickery, could be illusion, or it could be hell itself. Discern well."

Gently, she opens the door in front of her. Glancing over her shoulder, I see an office interior. There are desks arranged in rows with screens between them. For some people this is hell, me included. Trapped to a pod all day would kill me off.

Sister Martha motions for Farra to move ahead of her and his team follow his command. Smoothly they take up different rows in the office and carefully search each pod. One officer gives a muffled hail to Farra. I turn and see the officer has found a boy and is beginning to lead him towards Sister Martha.

The nun looks carefully at the boy before reaching out a hand

and grabbing the child by the throat. With blinding speed she snaps his neck before letting him drop to the floor. The officer stares at her in shock and Farra trains his weapon on her. But she merely steps away. Looking down the corridor, I see where the boy should be lying on the floor. There's something there, something, but it's not human.

"Remember, discern well."

A chill runs through me on hearing her warning. Of course I have seen this sort of illusion at firsthand but it scares me no less for that. Carefully, I creep to the window of the office and see I am about five floors up from the ground. In the street below there is a ground swell of people, a mass of clamoring misfits. There are people here from all walks of life but all seem to be hungering to get to the front of the crowd.

At the head of the crowd stands a redhead in a monk's habit that flaps in the breeze exposing too much. She laughs as she pours the contents of a cup down the throats of those assembled. As they spasm and wretch on tasting, she mocks them before watching them transform. There's a hunger in the eye, a snarl on the mouth and an urgency to seek someone or something. And then they bound off.

So this is it, the place where they will launch their attacks. Without getting too close to the glass I try to scan the street but I cannot recognize the place. However the district is obvious. Edelweiss.

"Come on," says Sister Martha, "we have ground to cover." Making our way to the stairs in the middle of the floor, Farra sends his team first. They move so quietly and with minimal hand signals. I hear the quiet click of a rifle and then walk past a bleeding body on the floor. Sister Martha barely acknowledges it. I've never seen her quite like this. There's an urgency and a determination but underneath, she's scared, truly scared.

"Where are we going?" I ask Martha as we stop by a doorway.

"Deeper into the stronghold."

"Yes, but where? We are in Edelweiss."

"Yes," says the Sister, "but there is more than Edelweiss here. At some point we shall step into his realm. To keep himself protected he stands in hell. Like an embassy on our earth. The American embassy in Australia is American soil and so the place where the demon is, is a part of hell."

"And you fear going there?" I ask.

"So should you. I doubt I will be coming back."

"Isn't that a bit defeatist?"

"You don't get it yet, Detective. I didn't fight a first battle and lose. I have been in constant battle on a different plane. Constantly I have been worn down, constantly attacked. Father Krystanovic's death is replayed to me, taunted at me, his belief that I betrayed him. I am ready to go on, Detective, ready to go home. But this must be done."

"Quiet!" says Farra in a hushed whisper.

He's indicating that there's some sort of trouble at the base of the stairs. I shuffle up to him and he lets me peak through a barely open door. There are a number of monks in habits milling around the floor beyond the door. There's no way to sneak out past them and if we simply open fire we'll bring everyone to us. Sister Martha was insistent we don't make a noise until we reach the demon.

"Can we get out another way?" I ask Farra.

He shakes his head. "At some point we have to exit to the streets or we simply remain in this building. I doubt they are simply going to walk off."

Kobold is beside us and over hears. "I could lead them off,

give them the run around so you can continue."

"That's suicide," I say, looking at Farra. Sister Martha has turned around and places her hand on me.

"The child is brave but alone she would not distract enough away. She will need help. We need to split our forces and cause a distraction. Officer Farra?"

"Yes Sister, and it's Captain."

"Well Captain, send six of your men with Officer Kobold. Cause as much havoc as you can, dear." The Sister manages a smile but I can see it's forced.

"She's going nowhere without me." It's Hughes, ready with her shotgun.

"You have kids, Hughes," I protest but she waves me away.

"We all got someone Mulgrew. Stick him one from me."

I nod and step back to allow Farra's men to assemble. Kyla suggests those of us remaining retreat and find another set of stairs to emerge from and I agree. I tell Hughes to give us five minutes and then begin. Shaking her hand, I hope this isn't the last time I see her. Kobold looks so young and small beside Hughes but she's smiling, ready for the fray.

Once I have walked I don't look back, it would be too hard. Kyla touches my hand, acknowledging what I'm feeling before taking point. Moving quickly, we get across the building and down a second set of stairs. It seems like the tradesman's set, grubby and with occasional bits and pieces on the floor such as a bit of cardboard box.

We reach the door to the ground floor thirty seconds before the others will make their attack. My heart pounds and I try to stay composed. Sister Martha peers out of the gap in the door but she doesn't need to tell us when the others attack. Hughes' shotgun erupts and as we run through the door, we can see monks running to the far end of the building.

We are in the clear when a monk comes around the corner. Farra steps forward and dispatches him without drawing his weapon. He starts dragging the figure with him and then dumps it out of sight behind the stairs we emerged from.

I look back to see Hughes yelling as she empties her weapon once more. But then there's a shattering of glass. Something explodes into the building, sending shards everywhere and it lands with a beat of wings. It's black and at least twenty foot tall. With a mighty swing of an arm it sweeps some monks out of the way splattering them on the reaming glass panes.

Hughes fires but there's no effect. I see one of the SWAT team being picked up and devoured. My instinct is to help but Sister Martha grabs my arm.

"They are gone Trimble. Run. We need to run."

Chapter 35

"What was that?" I ask as we halt around a street corner.

"One of hell's spawn, Detective. Best not to dwell on it. That's what it wants you to do, to take it in and affect your mind," says Sister Martha.

"But it just ate him."

"Detective! I said don't dwell on it."

Kyla is at the head of the group and spins round to look for directions. She has a finger held up to her mouth telling me to shush and I nod back, suitably rebuked. With open arms, she asks Sister Martha where to go next. The nun appears to be contemplating but with no eyes the actual processes going on within her mind are hard to tell. Farra takes a walk to the front of the group and looks around the corner before us.

There's a smell of decay in the air, death, the same smell you would get in a morgue if they didn't keep it cool. A background din of chanting and yelling fills the air and there are a multitude of car alarms going off. I can taste smoke on my lips and I realize a faint fog is in the air. A lot of these tastes and sounds I have heard before, during riots in the city. But beyond these there is a sense of foreboding and high pitched shrieks and wails I cannot place. They send a chill up my back.

Kyla grabs my hand and I snap back to my senses. The Sister is at the corner and is indicating we should cross the street. Farra is on her shoulder and is hand signaling to his remaining men. They flank out and he wags his finger, telling us to run across.

Kyla goes first followed by Sister Martha. Kyla's dark hair bobbing about behind her in her ponytail is a redemptive sight and I watch her cross, finding this some sort of norm in this hell hole. But as soon as she reaches the other side, I begin to run, Gonzales on my tail. There's a dog now running towards me from my left hand side and I think about taking a shot as I see a set of ravenous teeth.

It's crazy as this is the type of dog, a Golden Retriever, that should adorn any family photograph but this one looks insane, like something rabid. It's bounding towards me at speed and seems to have only one intent. There are several faint clicks and the animal is thrown off its stride, blood spurting from it as it falls to the ground.

I try not to think but the image is frankly gross. My feet continue as fast as they can, almost on an auto-pilot, and I reach the building opposite. Kyla has the front glass door open and I rush inside to see Sister Martha striding into the back rooms. I'm breathing heavily but she appears to not require air as she looks like she's been sitting the whole time, not an ounce of sweat on her.

Behind me the door closes and I know Kyla has caught up on me when I feel a gentle smack on my bottom. Her face has a smile as she walks past which is such a contrast to the situation and I try to drink it in but then I notice the man in the corner of the room. He's lying crumpled, his arm at an angle nobody would have intended and half of his face is gone.

My mind is brought right back to our situation.

Sister Martha leads us through the back rooms to an alleyway. With a quick glance down the passage, we cross to a plain fire door at the back of the building opposite. Farra has it opened in seconds and we step inside before he seals it up behind us. There's little light and I follow Sister Martha's back until she takes us into a passage, basic and bare, like the back parts of a supermarket. There's the occasional fire notice or warning sign but otherwise it is bare concrete.

As we make our way down this new passage, the nun takes a sharp turn to a door on our left and we enter what looks like the staff canteen. It's a mess with food everywhere and blood on the tables. Looking along the floor I see several bodies. If I didn't believe we were walking into hell before, I am convinced. Everywhere is just death and destruction. Quickly we move through the destroyed restaurant and join another corridor before we see a door that leads out onto the supermarket floor. There are the usual rows of stacked goods but many have been taken down, thrown onto the floor with a degree of anger, and liquids and solids are on the floor.

Farra indicates we pair up to cross the supermarket floor and I feel Kyla tap my ass before whispering in my ear "Let's go, Tiger." It's trite and maybe not entirely appropriate given the sights we have been seeing but she knows how to pick me up. I follow her down an aisle of cereal products, carefully trying to avoid anything going crunch beneath our feet. The lights of the supermarket are still on and there's the occasional trolley left in the aisles.

Kyla's down low, focused on the junction ahead, I think it's where the tinned soups meets the breads. But I can hear a sound like a slither. There's a fishy smell to accompany it and

I hear some tins hit the hard floor. Kyla looks around but like me I doubt she sees anything odd.

And then it happens. My leg is whipped out from behind me and I slam into the supermarket floor, suddenly being dragged backwards. I yell out to Kyla who turns and fires at something behind me. Once, twice. But there's a tentacle on the floor behind her. Deep purple with suckers on the inside, like those of an octopus.

I see the tentacle start to reach for her foot and I scream out a warning. But she is caught unaware as her leg is lifted and she is flipped upside down, the tentacle holding her inverted. As I slide backwards to whatever doom is behind me, I see her flailing, her weapon falling from her hands. As the tentacle takes her around the corner of the aisle, I catch a glance at her horrified face.

I want to get up and run, go and get her back but I continue backwards. Now she is out of sight I force myself to turn over so that I can see my attacker. Round the end of the aisle I slide, shoulder catching a corner hard, causing me to yelp. But I am silenced quickly as a multitude of teeth come into sight. Row upon row of hideous sharp canines, with drool pouring amongst them, are only a matter of twenty feet away.

I try for purchase, reaching for anything I can hold onto. My hand finds a piece of shelving which cuts into my skin but I grip tight. My leg is pulled hard and I swear it'll pop out of its socket. Trapped in a hellish limbo, my mind scrambles for other ideas. But then my hand slips and I am dragged towards the chomping teeth.

Chapter 36

I prepare to throw everything I have at the approaching teeth, desperately summoning up the courage to kick out hard and throw whatever punch I can. But a number of clicks cut the air, and bullets ricochet off the teeth before several of the white incisors break off causing green liquid to spray into the air. A figure appears beside me and fires into the tentacle holding me and I fall to the floor.

My shoulder hits the ground first and I am hauled to my feet by the black clad SWAT member who indicates I should run back down the aisle I was dragged along. I turn to thank him but watch in horror as he is grabbed by another tentacle, his weapon falling from his hands to the floor and before I can speak he is whipped to those teeth ,which immediately begin to feast on him.

I turn my back from the sight and reach down for his weapon. Rage building inside me, I spin back around and begin to discharge the rifle into the creature. I can barely look at it and I scream out loud, letting go every bullet in the magazine. But it has a silencer and it's a weird sensation as my voice is clear above the quiet click of the rounds passing through.

A hand grabs my shoulder and I am turned around into the eyeless face of Sister Martha.

"Stop it, you fool, or we will all die right here. We go."

Her hand is unbelievably strong on my shoulder and I am half dragged along to the far end of the supermarket floor. But there's a sickening feeling in my stomach, a sudden despair that cannot be stopped.

"Kyla? Where is Kyla?"

"I don't know Detective, I really don't know but we cannot go back. None of us matters, only destroying that creature of hell. We go on, Detective. We go!"

I hold my ground. "No! She's back there with that thing. She needs me."

"She needs you to go and kill a demon! Otherwise there's nothing. Do you understand? There's nothing."

"That might be your orders but that's Kyla, that's one of our own, she's mine. You understand, she's mine. I can't leave her."

The Sister shakes her head. "Then we are doomed. Give me the knife. I shall have to kill it. I need you in this showdown, Detective, you would not be here otherwise."

"Take the others. I'm going back for her."

The Sister purses her lips and then points at Farra and his team. Gonzales tries to follow me but I stop him. "Go with the Sister and do what you can. I'll catch you up."

He looks at me as if beaten but turns away to follow the Sister, and I watch them exit quickly through the side door. My mind is racing and I walk down an aisle full of gardening equipment, picking up an axe on the way. No doubt it's pretty blunt but I am weaponless.

Scanning the store, I see a little piece of black above an aisle and make my way there. From a distance it looks like the back of her hair, pulled tight in that wonderful ponytail she favors and I know I'll see her neck soon. There's a sense of hope, thankfulness and I whisper out her name. But she doesn't reply so I sneak up behind her quickly, not wanting to alert anything else but with a heart that's leaping with joy.

I touch her shoulder but she doesn't react. So I tap her hard but again no reaction. My heart is now beating fast for a different reason and I grab her shoulder turning her around.

Where the face should be is a mass of snakes which strike out at me. I fall backwards and start scrabbling clear, one hand still on my axe. Everything looks like Kyla except this front face that has no features, just a black recess and these damn snakes.

Where is she? What have they done to her? I keep pushing back on the floor as this thing approaches me. I look at the snakes, fangs protruding and small black eyes staring at me. There's must be at least fifty of them coming out of the void on her face.

This is not Kyla! This is not Kyla! I repeat the mantra over and over in my head until I feel strong enough to get to my knees. The creature senses I am weak and makes a lunge for me. Stooping away from the snakes, I swing the axe low and it bites into the kneecap, knocking the creature over and down. Rising, I follow up by raining blows down upon it, trying not to look at the damage I am causing.

This is not Kyla! This is not Kyla! I drop the axe not wanting to look at the blood. This is not Kyla! I need to find her. I walk the aisles of the supermarket looking for the tentacle creature but it's not here. I scour the floor, desperately looking for a route it might follow.

There's a small run of slime heading back into the rear of the shop and I follow it. As I reach a set of double doors, I see a small hair tie on the floor. It's simple, plain black. I've seen her use the tie to wrap her hair up so many times. This is one of hers, I know it.

I push open the doors and continue to follow the trail of slime. It leads down a corridor to an outside door. Listening to the outside world, I hear the yells and cries but nothing that sounds like it is in the immediate area.

Gingerly, I open the door and look into the face of a monk dressed in a black habit. My knee rises and catches him right between his legs. With my left hand, I grab him and drag him inside, pounding him with a right hook. I punch again and again until I see he is out cold. The hood of the habit has fallen back and I see a clean shaven man of maybe fifty. I turn away but something makes me stare at his face.

The hair is neatly cut and he looks like an office worker. There's nothing peculiar about his face, nothing that makes him look like a movie star but he's not ugly either. In almost every way he is just a normal guy but dressed in a monk's habit, worshipping a demon and ready to inflict untold evil on his fellow citizens. Inside my world is rocking. I always thought these people were somehow different, somehow abnormal. But I reflect that most I have come across are average Joes and that is the most terrifying thing about this whole crappy mess.

Focus Kyle, focus. Kyla, we need to get to Kyla.

Chapter 37

I listen again at the door, and happy that the area outside is clear, I open the door a little more carefully this time and see a clear alleyway. Across from me is a tall building of which several floors appear to be on fire. As a rule I don't like fire, as it burns and leaves a mark you don't get rid of easily, but the trail of slime is heading into that building. After a quick look left and right, I run over to the door opposite at the foot of the building.

It's locked and I don't hang about. I run around the building until I see a second door and carefully open it. Inside there is a corridor with a pale green emulsion on the wall. It looks like sick and probably something we would get at the station.

There's a set of stairs heading up, for the corridor ends in a door. Walking to the door, I hear voices, well, noises at least. They may be voices but not human voices. Funny how that doesn't seem like a weird phrase anymore. Still, I don't want to get too close, especially if that's not where Kyla is.

I turn back and take the stairs. One flight up there's another door and I listen. Nothing. Opening the door, I see a corridor with glass panels along it, offering a view into a large number of desks all neatly arranged. It looks like a call center, quite apt for being in hell. I can't see anyone moving but there is definitely commotion on the floor above.

Turning back I climb another flight of stairs. Again I find another empty set of offices but I notice that the ceiling is bowing. Satisfied there's no one on this level, I climb another flight and this time the door is hot to touch. Holding the handle with my jacket, I crack it open slightly. The heat is palpable. Inside there's an orange tinge to everything and the ceiling is missing. A group of monks are on this floor and seem to be looking up and chanting, lost in whatever sight is higher up.

I'm assuming that the something up there cannot be good and I sneak carefully across the floor and crouch behind a panel of what used to be a section of corridor. Looking up, I can see a number of winged creatures, long talons on the ends of their four arms and a single nail, almost bladelike, on their foot. I say foot but that's only because that's what they are hanging upsidedown from. Maybe it's a claw but there's a human aspect to it as it seems to join an ankle.

While I'm sure many zoologists may find this an interesting study, all I feel is a need to stay well clear of them. At least there are no tentacles here, whatever these creatures are. But then something catches my eye. High up, hanging, there appear to be people.

I shift round, ending up under a table and then juking out to catch a glimpse of the predicament of these fellow humans. There's a whole new perspective opening up in my mind when I realize that multiple species doesn't just refer to the animal kingdom. There appears to be a number of men and women in various states of pain. Some move and some don't. But one catches my eye.

The black leather jacket, the jeans, the loose hair splayed across her shoulders, all these are signs but the real giveaway is how she seems to be fighting her bonds, struggling to get out. Hold on, Kyla, I'm coming.

Because of how high she is above me I am struggling to decide how to rescue her. At first, my thoughts are to find a weapon and shoot her bonds but at this distance I'd probably shoot her. On the other hand, I am going to struggle at heights, as they are not my forte, more a curse to me. But I suppose there's nothing for it.

Awaiting my chance, I lie in cover counting the floors I need to go up. Seven. Just the seven. And even then I'm not sure if I can reach her. But I see her struggle and try to kick out which causes her to swing and grimace as her bonds cut into her. I need to hurry.

With the monks facing away, I go back to the corridor and then the stairwell. Whilst keeping a lookout, I go as quick as I can, taking two steps at a time, like some sort of gangly antelope. If I lived in the bush with my grace, I wouldn't survive a day. There's nothing on the way up except the occasional dump of excrement. I assume it's excrement, not because it looks like any I know but because it stinks to high heaven.

On reaching the seventh floor up, I carefully open the door and gaze into the corridor beyond, or rather what remains of it. Half of the passage is gone, wall ripped away and only pieces of jutting floor remain. There's a thin track to walk and even that has places where there are just beams grimly holding on.

I make my way onto the narrow passage and have to pin myself to the door as a shadow sweeps past. It's one of the creatures but I don't think it saw me. At least I guess it didn't as it hasn't come back for me. Having no cover, I continue quickly until I reach a connecting wall and find some remnants of concrete to hide behind. Peering over, I find a heartening sight.

Kyla is only a few feet away, hanging by her bonds but most definitely alive and kicking. She's twisting and turning, trying to free her wrists from some sort of tacky lace that holds her. The lace is stuck onto beams above, not wrapped, but like it has been affixed with some incredibly strong glue.

My problem is how do I get her clear, how do I free her? I'm not sure I have anything that could cut through the lace and she doesn't look like she's about to be freeing herself any time soon. I'm also aware that if I step out and take too long, I will be standing seven floors up without a parachute and attracting the attention of things that can actually fly.

When the one you love is suffering and you don't know what to do, it is a hell all of its own. She needs me now and I find myself being almost useless. I turn my back to try and concentrate, trying to keep the vision of her struggling from my mind while I think this through logically but it's only partially successful.

And then she screams and I can feel a wind passing over me. Turning back to Kyla, I look over the piece of wall and have to squint my eyes as dust fills the air. Through the maelstrom I can make out one of the winged creatures hovering in front of Kyla and cutting the lace that binds her. With one of its arms, it holds Kyla while using its talons to cut her free.

I panic, not knowing if she will be taken away or simply killed. Images of her being dropped or eaten come to mind and there's a cold sweat on my brow. Without a thought to how my actions are going to help, I hurdle the low piece of wall, take four steps along a beam and fling myself at the creature.

My hands desperately clutch at it and I grab a wing causing it to tighten in against the creature's body. There's an unholy screech and a yell from Kyla before we drop. Like a roller-coaster ride, we race straight down and my stomach is left in the clouds.

Chapter 38

The creature is struggling like mad but I have a firm grip on its wing. We spin as we fall and I hear it flap the other wing causing our fall to slow slightly. But it's no time before we hit the floor, the creature's body slamming hard into the ground and I tumble off it, avoiding the hardest impact.

Rolling to my feet and still rather groggy, I look for Kyla. She has been let go and is lying on the floor, her hands still bound. I run over and pick her up by the shoulder. She yelps with the pain but works her feet from under her and we sprint for the side of the large room. Above us, I hear wings flapping and unholy cries to the air.

Wary of the threat from above, I make for the corridor at the side but several monks step across to stop us. The first gets a boots in his nuts and I head-butt the second hard causing blood to splatter everywhere. Kyla double hands another with her clasped fists and is then grabbed by another. She bites him hard and he lets go and gets a foot driven into the back of his knee, followed by a blow to the head.

The winged creatures are coming down onto us and we dive behind a pillar holding up the corridor. The creatures are too large for the corridor itself and I see talons raking into the void and press myself up against the wall.

"If we stand still, we're dead," I tell Kyla and she nods, starting to edge along the corridor wall. Quickly, we slide along before exiting via the door. There's no real thought, just a panic mode and we flee the building into the street. I turn left away from the previous building I had been in and down an alleyway at the end of which I can see monks with their backs to us.

"Inside that door," says Kyla. She barges the plain door and it opens sending her tumbling into a dark corridor with a red light at the end. I follow and quickly close the door behind me. Picking Kyla up, we race along in the darkness until a door opens in front of us. A giant of a man stands before us, at least seven foot tall. He wears a suit but carries an automatic weapon.

"Don't move," snorts the man before saying over his shoulder, "boss we got two normals here. And the bird's not bad either."

"Bring them in," comes the voice and I recognize it.

"Louis, Louis, I never thought I'd be glad to hear your voice," I say.

"Well, well, if it isn't everyone's favorite detective. What the hell is all this Trimble? It's just not safe to be on the street today."

The big man ushers us in and looks to frisk me. I give him a look before his boss says, "Today he's the good guy, Vito. There's nothing to fear from him today. Sit down Trimble. Who's your companion?"

I walk into the room and see many large red sofas occupied by a variety of women wearing very little and all looking rather frightened. Louis Colhorne is sitting on the largest sofa, a woman on either side with his arm around each one. I take a pew on the couch opposite and Kyla sits beside me. I can tell she's not impressed with the surroundings.

"Louis, meet Detective Kyla Corstain, helped me with the last bit of business of this nature."

"Obliged, Ma'am," says Louis. "But I think you only pissed them off. They seem to be back in numbers."

"More than you know Louis. I take it this is one of your knocking…, sorry houses of entertainment. I'm afraid you picked a bad time to be here, Louis."

He steps over to Kyla and takes a switchblade from inside his jacket. He tries to cut the bonds on Kyla's wrist but it's too tough for the knife.

"What the hell, Trimble? What is this shit?"

"I suggest we try to shoot it off, if you have a silencer. We really don't want to attract attention."

"Vito, like the man says."

The giant man helps Kyla to her feet, delicately to be fair, and takes her to the corner of the room. She holds her wrists out and he positions himself behind her and his handgun, complete with silencer, on the bonds. There's a click and a snap as the bond breaks.

"Thank you," says Kyla and rolls her wrists. I try to make sure she's okay but she waves away attention.

"I'd pass an inappropriate comment Trimble but I reckon you're sweet on this one," says Louis.

"He's more than that," says Kyla, and she pulls her jacket down tight in a motion that says she's more than fine, ready to go.

"So what's the deal Trimble? When you guys going to get this under control?"

"Louis," I say, "I really don't know if we will. You might laugh but this is hell itself being let loose. It's a demon setting up his throne and if we don't get to him and end him then it's all over. I mean everything."

"You're not shitting me, Trimble, are you?"

I shake my head and Louis becomes sullen. "Always the same, work your way up and some asshole tries to take top spot. Would we lose the city?"

"The city," spits Kyla, "we lose everything. City, country, family, everything."

"You seem a bit of a small force, Trimble."

"Louis, we had SWAT, Kobold and others I value. But it's been crazy to get to here and there's a long way to go. I ain't even armed at the moment."

"Well I can help there. Vito, get them both a gun from the armory, something potent."

"Have you got anything big down there?" asks Kyla.

"Big?"

"Bazooka, something really destructive?" Louis looks a little taken aback and seems to be thinking. "I don't care what it is and I don't care why you have it, man. We need heavy weaponry to survive here, so if you have it, get it the hell up here."

Kyla's in a rage. There's no quips about the women sat here, which would normally drive her nuts, no subtly, just demands. But she doesn't know Louis, and he likes to think he's the boss. I have an uneasy feeling.

"You pick them well, Trimble. Feisty with a body to match. You won't control this one, not like these ladies here." It's like he's baiting Kyla as he runs his hand across the ass of the girl on his left. "But okay, Detective Kyla Corstain, go with Vito. Whatever she wants Vito, bring them back up here."

Kyla follows the giant out of the room and Louis makes a

vulgar sign at me indicating what he thinks of Kyla. I let it slide, firstly because he is actually right, she is all that, but also because we need his help.

"So best I just hole up here then Trimble and let you sort this out. I'll keep these ladies well protected."

"The hell you will, Louis. Get all your men here and get packed to the gills with whatever weapons you can. You're going to help me get to this demon and then you're going to watch me kill it."

"And why's that Trimble?"

"One, you need to or you'll die. Two, if you don't I'll give some of these girls a weapon and let them have five minutes with your balls, and three, which you really don't want, I'll tell Corstain you are refusing to help."

Louis lets go a laugh and I know I've pitched it right. "But seriously, Louis, city needs you or this won't get done. You and me are on the same side at the moment, whether we like it or not."

Chapter 39

Kyla returns to the room with an automatic weapon hanging over her shoulder and I can see the rounds of ammunition in her pockets. She's followed by the giant who is carrying several wooden crates. A number of other men then enter with other boxes.

"Our friend seems to have been preparing for a war," says Kyla, "and thank God he did. There are automatics, handguns, rifles, grenades, and one that I'll be taking." She cracks open a crate the giant has set down and produces a small rocket launcher.

The absurdity of the scene is not lost on me as one of the women in the room comes over to Kyla and dressed in lingerie looks at the weapon. I'm sure there's an old style men's lifestyle magazine photographer who would wet himself at this image but for me it's the look Kyla throws at the woman that has me in fits of laughter.

"Do you know where this creep is?" asks Louis.

"Demon, Louis, it's a demon. Remember that. It'll trick, cheat you or just plain cut you apart if it wants to. And while this gear is all very helpful, we need to catch up with some friends of mine, who have a special weapon to kill it." Louis looks at me like I'm crazy. "Louis, when the last time happened

I took down a beast from somewhere other than this world. It nearly killed one of my SOCOs. So if you don't believe, fine, but you soon will."

I wait for Louis to gather all his men in the room and let Kyla give them a pep talk about not engaging until we have to. There's eight including Louis. Most are standard gang thugs but they look like they can handle themselves. Kyla gives them five minutes and then comes over, sitting beside me on a sofa.

"So all this flesh in the room, Kyle, you not tempted?"

I raise an eyebrow. "Turned on, of course. Tempted? No. I'm just thinking what outfit would suit you best."

She punches me in the side "Like the lingerie would even get a look in." Kyla calls one of the women over and I wonder what she's up to. I'd like to say I watch her approach with utter dispassion but I'm male, so that ain't happening. But Kyla whispers something in her ear and the woman disappears briefly before returning and offering something in her hand. Kyla takes the simple band and I watch her bunch her hair and apply the hair tie, showing off that neck that can grab me from half a mile away.

"You own me," I whisper in her ear, taking the chance to nuzzle her neck. She nods and stands, looking down at me.

"Get me through this and you can pick the lingerie," she teases.

"Like you said, the lingerie won't get a look in." She smiles but for all our teasing the fear is in her eyes. Don't get me wrong, she's resolute as ever but there's a fear.

"As I said before, where is this creep, or demon as you insist?" Louis had been there the whole time but I guess he's wise enough not to interrupt or comment. I reckon he's grasped the seriousness of the situation even if he doesn't fully comprehend.

"Well, Louis, it gets complicated. You see its world is breaking into ours, a sort of convergence. Don't ask beyond that, my expert's missing. But we have an ace to find where it is. It wants Corstain, and more than that, she can sense him. It laid a hand on her, a proper hand, and it has left a mark."

"Can't blame it for that," says Louis.

There's a slap across his cheek and Kyla is inches from him. "Don't ever talk about that. You can parade your women, you can do whatever filth you do on the streets but my body and what happens to me is off limits."

There are eight guns pointing at Kyla. Actually there are seven, one is pointing at me. I must keep an eye on the guy doing that because he's got a bit of sense. Louis is staring at Kyla and then at me.

"Use words next time, toots. I don't take kindly to over aggressive women." There's a fall in the tension and I breathe out. Kyla turns away and pretends to check some ammunition as Louis comes back to me.

"I like her, Trimble. If you can't handle her send her my way."

"I don't think Kyla's the sort you handle, Louis." I smile inwardly. She just keeps digging further and further into me. Like I wasn't sold before. "When it touched her, it left not just a physical mark but a mental connection. She's heard it and felt it when close. In an intimate way. Like it never left her. So she's our antenna and our bait.

"But I warn you Louis, don't piss her about if it's reaching out to her, if it's causing her any pain. She'll blow your balls off. And if she can't, I will. I respect you and I need your help, but that would be a line too far."

He simply nods and then turns to his men. He probably

realizes I don't respect him but it's what his sort say to each other. I do need him though. But not the ladies who I advise to get some clothing on, stay in the room and barricade the doors when we are gone. I tell Louis to leave them some weapons too, although how far that will get them, who knows. I'd escort them away but there's no time.

Kyla has the rocket launcher over her shoulder and two hand guns at her side. I've an automatic rifle and a handgun but I feel under armed. We need the knife Sister Martha has. She'll be heading towards the demon, so that's our play, hunt around until Kyla finds, is contacted by or feels the demon in a stronger way.

"Let's go," says Louis and turns to Kyla. "Blow his ass to kingdom come, toots. Dude doesn't know how to treat a lady."

I can feel Kyla's rage at his hypocrisy, surrounded by scantily clad women, some probably here under duress of some sort. But she gives a nod. Only a nod mind, no smile. She saves that for when she looks at me. You can keep your speeches, your great war cries, all this baloney about King and country. Save for perhaps the image of his children, there is no greater spur for a man about to undergo hell than the image of the woman he's fighting for. Especially if her hair's tied up. Yeah, I know, I'm obsessed, that's the point surely.

"Good evening, ladies. Gentlemen, if you will kindly follow my partner, we shall commence hostilities." I watch Kyla stride off down the corridor. There's no greater fear than to know your woman is entering that hell with you.

Chapter 40

From the rear of the party, I see Kyla at the front door with Louis, gingerly opening it up. Her head pops out for a moment and then the door swings open and we all run out into the street. Normally as police officers we would run to the cover, looking at the various points of protection the enemy might be using. But Louis doesn't operate like that, and is flanked by his men. Well, he's certainly got attitude.

I really don't fancy trying to operate with one of these goons and so I run hard to catch up with Kyla and work as a team. There's a smile when she sees me alongside and then an automatic drop into "cover and move", our method of ensuring we are not exposed when there's little protection.

The air is filled with the noise of a riot and cries from things that I'm not sure even exist. I catch a glance of Louis' face and can see he's unsettled. I guess in his rabbit warren it was easy to pretend nothing much was happening but now with the full story he looks spooked.

A winged creature, sleek and black swoops down from above and grabs one of Louis' men in its claw. Before it can fly away, Louis is unloading a barrage of bullets into its side. Kyla drops on one knee and joins in the frenzy. The creature bucks and twists but still stands. It rises to fly but its wings get torn to shreds and it starts to collapse.

The man who was grabbed is screaming out until the creature in a wild turn simply tosses the man out of its claw. He sails through the air down the street beyond us and I see his body disappear behind a car. He doesn't emerge.

"Bastard black bird," shouts Louis and continues to fire until the creature topples backwards. "See that Trimble, so much for your demon."

"That's its pet, Louis, you ain't met the boss yet." I find the concern for his man somewhat lacking. He's probably dead and part of me feels we should check but really, what are we going to do? Having been thrown through the air like that, he's probably broken nearly every bone in his body if he's still alive. We can hardly get an ambulance. We'd probably just be putting him out of his misery.

I clear the thought from my mind. "Nice and noisy though Louis, I expect we'll see more soon. We need to be off the street, move with a bit more decorum and discretion. Subway's round that corner. We'll make for that."

Kyla's already ahead of me and she takes up point on the corner as I approach her side. "You okay?" I ask.

"Great. And you?" I smile. "You're still thinking about me in that lingerie."

"Nah," I reply, "Thinking about you without it."

"Well then, keep me well covered and your luck might be in." With that she runs off to the next point of cover behind a fruit stall. It's totally inappropriate and probably in bad taste but I feel good. Her promise is driving me on. How fickle we are.

One of Louis' men is suddenly grabbed by a tentacle that explodes from a window and hauls him inside. I'm about to shout that they shouldn't follow when it dawns on me they are all running away from the occurrence. So much for loyalty and camaraderie. Still it's the smart move.

Kyla rushes to the subway entrance and drops to her knee, looking back and covering my route. As I run forward to join her at the gated entrance to the subway, I can see a man rushing towards her from behind. She hasn't clocked him and he seems wild, like those who have drunk the blood.

"Kyla!" I scream and she turns but too late. The man swipes an arm at her and she falls to the ground. Running towards her, I pull my shotgun but the man is already being peppered by Louis and his automatic rifle. I watch the man jerk and then bounce off the wall falling to the ground. Louis turns to me, triumph in his eyes.

But I look beyond him, knowing how these possessed people are and see the man begin to stand. There's daylight through him in patches and he's now ignoring Kyla. Instead he's running for Louis. I shout a warning and drop to my feet, shotgun held against my shoulder.

I've not got the best aim in the world but sometimes you have no choice. The man is close to Louis and there's no time. His hands are upstretched as Louis starts to turn around and suddenly recognizes his plight.

Weapons can fire so quickly. One minute there was a face full of rage, the next, no head at all. Louis is in shock, covered in red fluid. For a moment I see Louis almost retch but then he recovers himself, laughing at the scene around him. "You know how to ruin a good suit, Trimble." That is one sick attitude. But then, he has killed for fun.

Racing to Kyla, I see her getting back to her knees. Her mouth's bloody but she's got a look of determination on her face. "Subway, Kyle, Subway."

I nod and she turns to the locked gate that protects the entrance to what is described as Parkton station. From my days on the beat, I remember it's small with the two lines passing through in either direction. I draw my handgun and shoot the lock off before kicking open the gates. There's no light beyond the first few flights of steps I can see and I hope no one has been down here as it will make our route easier if nothing has been attracted to this point.

Together, Kyla and I run down the steps, eyes glued to the darkness. I hear Louis and his goons following and I shout for them to lock the gates as best they can. "What with?" shouts Louis but I leave that to his improvisation.

The bottom of the stairs turns to a long corridor that descends down several flights of steps at various points but there is nothing about. As we reach the last descent, we can make out the station beyond, lit up with emergency lighting. It's dim and I sneak a look before walking out onto the empty platform.

Kyla follows and I turn to her, asking her for some directions. She stands and clutches her chest and I can see she's being tormented at least on a mental level if not spiritual and physical. But she didn't hesitate to reach out and find her molester, our demon. After a few moments, she comes over and points down one of the tracks and I nod. She then clings to me, hands gripping me tight. "Tell me I'm yours," she says in a whisper.

"Always," I answer. "It doesn't own you."

"No," she says, "it bloody doesn't. But it's still under my skin. You need to banish it."

I nod wondering exactly how I do that. Does she mean right now? Is she talking about killing the demon? I'm holding her neck in my hand but I really don't know what she needs just now.

"Knock it off," says Louis, "I'm sure there'll be a room later. Which way, lady?"

Kyla points off in the direction she had advised me. Without waiting, Louis tells his men to follow and I go to admonish him, to stamp my authority. But Kyla shakes her head.

"Something's that way," she says. "Let him meet it first."

I look at her, almost disgusted that she would send Louis ahead with no warning. But she is determined that we should.

"All those girls, all the bad things he has done. Our demon's down those tracks, Kyle, but there's something awaiting us, I can feel it. Let Louis face it. I ain't losing you, that piece of shit can take the brunt." I thought she had been cool around Louis but it ran deeper than I thought. Maybe it's the bloke in me that missed it, maybe I think too much of her. I want to argue but I can't. If it's coming then there's no one deserves it more than Louis.

Chapter 41

There's no power down in the subway tunnel once we are clear of the platform. From the rear of the party, I can see Louis up ahead, casually striding forward, one of his men using their mobile phone as a makeshift torch. The light is impressive for such a small device but it casts a very dim glow to see by.

Kyla's walking beside me, a grim look on her face. Usually I can get a smile from her but she's determined yet worried. She's still got an automatic rifle in her hands and she seems to think whatever is ahead will require a large amount of fire power. I'm still struggling with letting an ally walk right into the brunt of something horrible but if I tell Louis, he'll have Kyla and me at the front.

His men are quiet although Louis is making up for them. He's constantly going on about pulverizing the winged creature, how he emptied his magazine into it. Admittedly, the amount of firepower displayed was very effective but I have a feeling that these creatures are not the real problem. And saying that scares me because they have already been a problem.

The track ahead curves before us to the right and I glance behind looking for a little light but the station has long disappeared. Here and there an emergency light displays, obviously run on a battery, but again it's more indicative of the sign rather than providing any useful light.

And then I hear a scurrying from up ahead. Quiet at first then beginning to build like it's being added to. The first sound was a distinctive tap of feet of some sort. But then it was like more feet were added. It's now becoming a din, resounding throughout the tunnel. But up ahead, there's nothing to see, nothing in the dark.

"You heard anything like this before," shouts Louis over the din.

"No, keep a good lookout."

"I doubt I'll miss these things with the din they are making." He laughs loudly, swinging his rifle around. I stare off into the distance seeking out where the noise is coming from until a thought dawns on me. It sounds like a horde of scurrying insects or some sort. Something small, like you would hear in one of those zoo houses for creepy crawlies and that. It sends a shiver down my skin as I don't really like that type of thing.

And then I see movement in the distance. Very blurred but definite movement, rapid and constantly changing like a rough sea. There are large bodies and many legs, at least I think they are legs, it's such a blur it's hard to tell. Many legs, big bodies. And coming along the roof.

"Louis, above!" I shout out but it's too late. From the ceiling falls a black blur and I hear Louis crying out. It's followed by another and another. I fire up into the ceiling as a black mass comes into view, all racing along. Before me, I see Louis' men becoming entangled and wrapped around, their faces disappearing, literally surrounded by fangs and a gaping hole.

"Get out of here," Kyla yells and I run to the side of the tunnel. There's a door there and I pull down on the emergency tunnel.

In the dark, I stumble on the steps and feel Kyla grab my collar. With the door open, we fall inside before Kyla fires back at the door. There's a splatter of wetness, like a blender going off half-cocked and I struggle to get back up to shut the door. Fortunately Kyla has the presence of mind and strength to reach forward and slam the door shut.

"What the hell?" shouts Kyla, as the metal door dings at the scrabble of arachnid limbs.

"Keep moving," I say, "there's no guarantee that'll hold." She pulls me up and I follow her down the narrow corridor, some type of engineer's passage between lines or some sort of quick access. "I can't believe they went down so quick."

"Serves the dirty sod right."

"Kyla!" All I get back is a dirty look and I don't push it. There's a real edge coming over her and it's not just the most recent situations. The whole place is doing something to her. Or maybe it's the connection with the demon worming its way into her psyche and make-up but she's being brutally cold. Not that Louis didn't deserve it.

"Are we still going the right way?" I ask.

"If you mean am I feeling his grip on my body increasing, then yes. I can feel him all over me. Kyle, he's practically enveloping me."

Looking at Kyla I don't see anything physically grabbing her, no reaction from her body but the grind of her teeth and the desperation in her eyes tells me what I need to know. I take her hand, a seemingly futile gesture but it seems to pick her up.

"Right," she says as we reach a fork in the corridor. "And up, we need to go up." Fortunately, there are stairs rising and we race up them until we reach another metal door. I stop and listen at it, hearing the noise of a city in turmoil, of yells and screams, the crackle of fire and the cries of the injured.

"Close, I think we're close." Kyla nods her agreement and for the first time clutches her chest as if someone has grabbed her. She shouldn't be here but no one could stop her.

I open the metal door and look outside into a scene from hell itself. I can see bodies on the floor everywhere, creatures dancing, people laughing and torment happening all around. The cityscape seems to have disappeared and there's now ledges of rock and a molten lake in near sight.

"Is this real?" shouts Kyla above the din.

"I don't know, and I don't care. Where is it? And where is Martha? She has the knife, we need Martha."

"I don't know," yells Kyla, "but I'm sensing him that way, towards the lake, the molten lake. Dear God, Kyle, it's on fire."

"Come on then. That way."

"Wait Kyle, wait!"

"What?" I shout.

"Can you hear that?" I shake my head. "It's the Sister, it's Martha, she's calling us, calling you."

I stop and listen, trying to screen out the cacophony of noise around me. But there's nothing.

"From that way," says Kyla pointing.

"It could be a trap," I say.

"But we need the knife, Kyle, we haven't got a choice. There's no option."

Indeed there isn't. Without the knife, according to the good Sister, we are dead in the water. I try to listen again but I'm getting nothing. "Take me to her, Kyla, I'm hearing nothing."

She nods and then grimaces. I see her body jerk and know he's reaching into forbidden parts, in her mind too. Shaking it off with a grimace, Kyla runs forward as if she's unsure her legs will stay upright.

We leave the rockscape before us and instead begin to run into a small tunnel, with dripping wet walls. There's symbols on the wall I don't recognise but I swear I can feel evil from them. I try not to linger on them but instead follow Kyla, concentrating on her as it moves down the passage. It breaks into a cavern after a short distance and as I gaze around the dark interior I catch a glimpse from the poor light of a nun's habit.

But as much as my heart jumps in anticipation of finding the Sister, it drops as a Serpentine creature spins around and makes its way to me. At over six feet, it's my largest snake. I can see the fangs dripping with fresh blood. Drawing my shotgun, I discharge and reload, noticing that the creature seems undisturbed by the physical violence done to it.

As it continues forward, I watch it slither towards Kyla and grab her leg with its tale. As it's about to strike, I pull the trigger to find the shotgun is jammed. Kyla screams as the creature strikes down.

Chapter 42

There's a heart stopping moment as the creature dives forward with its fangs and I watch Kyla roll violently to the left. The creature rears again but I have lost all of my entrancement and have run straight at it, leaning forward, hitting it just below the head and knocking it sideways. I roll off and scramble away as quick as I can, my back to it. On instinct, I zigzag my run as if someone is about to shoot at me and the head suddenly appears beside me, catching my rear and knocking me to the side. There's a pair of white fangs momentarily beside me before I keep rolling.

The snake rears, hissing loudly, causing me to look at the rear of its body where Kyla has started stabbing it with a small knife. Although the creature seems injured, it looks like it's more of a mild annoyance rather than a terminal blow. Standing, I run up behind the head and jump again onto its neck, grabbing onto its hood as the creature begins to rear this way and that.

In one hand I have a pen and the other is clinging on for dear life as I'm thrashed about. In a brief pause I throw myself further up and am able to reach forward to its eyes. Taking the pen, I stab it and hear it hiss wildly. Again it thrashes and I lose the pen. Grabbing now with both hands, I hang on desperately. But there's a sudden change. The creature now stops and turns its focus to Kyla, still held by the snake's tail.

With the pause, I climb forward again and see the one good eye the snake has left. This is going to be messy but Kyla's life will depend on it. I drive my hand into the good eye, pushing forward as hard as I can. The eye splits, goo flying everywhere and my hand sinks inside the head and I slip forward as the creature shakes its head. My arm is trapped and I'm hanging right before the fangs, swinging this way and that, the cold white teeth, dripping with what must be venom right before me.

The good side is the creature clearly cannot see and the pain caused has forced it to release Kyla who I see running away. My arm is in up to its elbow and I try to shake free but it's also the only limb supporting me. I feel like my shoulder might separate from myself and I try not to cry out, to not give this creature any frame of reference.

Then an idea strikes me as my nostrils fill with the foulest smell from the pus surrounding my arm. Turning my hand, I reach up and feel some spongey matter and squeeze. I hope it's the brain but in honesty I don't know. But whatever it is it means the snake isn't happy and suddenly drives its head to the ground where my legs first clatter into the rock surface before I'm able to find some purchase. I pull my arm clear with a hollow sucking sound and watery slop emerges soaking my legs. It stinks.

Kyla grabs my hand and pulls me away as the creature now starts to snap around with its fangs, blind to its enemies but keen to find them. The wet surface makes sprinting awkward but we clear the cavern for another tunnel leaving the wounded beast behind us. I look at Kyla and her face shows sheer disbelief but also pain. As we run on, she's clutching her chest.

"It's here," she yells, "It's all over me. Kyle get rid of it, get rid of it."

I put an arm round her in awkward fashion as we run along but I have no immediate answers. Get to Martha, get the dagger, and kill the son of a bitch. That's it, it's all I have.

"Martha? Do you still hear Martha?" I ask.

Kyla nods and leads on. But her face is in anguish. I try not to think about it as there's nothing I can do but it's hard to watch her suffer.

The tunnel keeps climbing and then breaks into a wooden paneled hall, complete with tapestries and paintings. But the images would disgust even Sketch and I try not to look. There's a door at the end of the room and Kyla points to it. And then she collapses.

I reach down and lift her head but her eyes are swimming. She's moaning and a fear is written all over her face, one of horror and repulsion. I don't know what it's doing to her but I'm livid, raging. But there's nothing I can do.

I pick her up and carry her to the door, depositing her gently on the wooden floor. My mind reels at this madness; molten rivers, slimy giant snakes, tentacles, creatures and stately rooms. I don't try to understand, I don't want to understand.

I hear voices inside the door. There's the calm voice of Sister Martha rebuking another speaker but my blood chills as the speaker replies. It's her, the redhead. It takes everything in me not to simply throw the door open and run in there to take her head off. But I'm weaponless now, everything gone in the fight with the snake.

Carefully I open the door and nearly gasp at the scene before me. Sister Martha is upside down, hanging by her feet with several cuts on her arms. She seems emotionless but she must be in agony. They've clearly beat her, and her face is a mass of blood and bruising. Around her are a group of maybe eight monks in their habits, facing Martha. A further glance inside the room reveals it's a circular chamber and there are several people tied up to the wall. Some look dead, certainly unconscious but one I see warms my heart. It's a tall woman, a strong Sergeant who takes no crap from anyone, Hughes. She's got one eye half closed and her face looks battered but she's conscious, her hands tied up above her.

I leave Kyla propped up against the wall outside the door before sneaking in while the redhead continues to rail against Martha.

"Where's Trimble? Where is he? And where's the bitch?" She's wild as she punches Martha, before kicking her in the face. My whole mind screams attack but I make my way round the edge of the wall, behind the backs of the monks and reach Hughes. There's a faint smile from her as I reach for her bonds. It's a poor knot but still takes me a minute to untie it and Hughes sensibly keeps her hands up above her head. Or maybe they are just stuck there.

"Where is he? I want him." The redhead, stands before Martha, her robe flailing and a bare leg snaking out. Her hood has now dropped and her hair flows freely. Such beauty contrasted with such hate. I'm almost entranced as she rails again punching Martha.

"Where is he? I want him, I want to have him and take him from her as my master defiles her. Where is he, you feeble bitch?"

"Right here," I yell and charge from the wall straight at her.

Chapter 43

I have the element of surprise but even so some of the monks manage to turn and try to block my path. I hit one with my shoulder driving him back as the other reaches for me, but his grasp fails and I drive on through towards Sister Martha. The monk on the end of my charge falls and I stumble up towards Martha to be met by a raking hand with painted red nails.

Swinging my head to the side, I watch the sharp appendages whizz past my face and I throw out an arm, grabbing hold of the redhead's ankle, upending her in the process. Her habit opens and I see she still hasn't grasped the idea of underwear.

"Up my back, Trimble," says Martha and I spin her round as she dangles reaching inside the rear of her garment. My hand finds an ornate dagger, one I remember. But the corner of my eye sees a redheaded monk that has righted herself and looks extremely pissed. And behind her are a number of other monks.

There's no time to cut Martha's bonds in an easy fashion and I simply jump and slash at the rope she is hanging from. The blade cuts with a sharpness I find astonishing and she falls head first to the ground. Thankfully she was only suspended two feet from the ground so although it's a good bump, it could have been a lot worse. I feel a hand on my arm as I land from my jump and turn to face a grimacing man in a monk's habit. My left hand has never been my strongest but it does have a mean left jab. And I punch quick and hard three times.

"Trimble, come here! Come here so I can have you, lust after me Detective."

I try to ignore the redhead's voice as more monks attack me and I throw jabs and kicks here and there. But it's like her voice isn't coming from her mouth but instead implanting into my brain. And it's drowning out all the background noise, so much so that I feel like I should be covering my ears. I start to twist with the pain of it and I get punched hard in my stomach. From a glance, I see her, habit flung open and hands on hips taunting me.

And then there's a shadow behind her, tall with broad shoulders. The mouth opens showing white teeth and a yell comes. A blow to the redhead catches her on the side of her cranium from behind and she falls. The voice stops instantly and I catch the sight of a laughing Hughes.

Someone has me round the neck and I drill my elbow into their stomach. Following up with another few elbows, I then double hand him to the face. The man falls and I run to Sister Martha who is rolling around on the ground after her fall. Steadying her, I slice the bonds holding her hands. But another monk is over me now and I look up into the hood of the habit. But there's nothing there. No face. Nothing, just an empty hood.

My heart jumps a beat and there's an inclination to just freeze, one that you get used to as a cop. But there's also an inner drive that comes with experience and I take the dagger and drive it into the habit. The clothing falls onto the weapon and it's like the body inside has just vanished. My hands are covered by the habit and I look down onto its flat surface.

And then comes the rake of nails I know too well, driven deep into my neck. I scream out in pain and a face comes before me licking its lips and making lewd comments to me. I try to grab her hands but I'm driven down with a punch from someone else. I haven't been able to account for everyone in the room and I cry out for Hughes to help.

The hands come off my neck. I fall over and look up at a bizarre sight. The redhead is being held up by the neck by a blind nun. Sister Martha is shaking her hard and the habit is being held closed by the nun as well.

"You have become filth, child. You have sullied yourself to it and fought to stop any help from all that is good. You were hurt but you chose to hurt. No more! No more!"

The Sister flings the redhead with a strength her body doesn't justify and the woman crashes off the far wall. An outstretched hand sends the remaining monks off their feet and into the wall as well.

"Get up Trimble! We need to stop it before it takes complete control."

I try to rise feeling unsteady on my feet. "Where are we?" I ask. "We were in Edelweiss. Where is this?"

"Pandemonium. Hell. Bedlam. Call it what you will it's their ground."

"And it's here in the city."

"No. Not yet. It is not yet established. We have crossed over to it. But the demon brings it closer now as blood is being spilt in the city. Things are blurred. Creatures are crossing over but the demon is not established. Not yet! We have to go and fast Trimble."

Rising, I feel Hughes giving me a hand and we stumble out of the room following the nun. I break off on exit and pick up Kyla who looks like she is in a delirium and one that's causing her a lot of pain.

"Leave her Trimble, she will slow us down on our hunt. You cannot help her other than defeat the demon. We must find it," says Sister Martha.

"But she'll find it. She's attached to it. It's doing whatever to her body. It's like she's being…"

"Grab her. And find the demon. Tell her we need to find it."

As a group we run back down the tunnels we came up, past a blind snake and then back to the heat and molten lake. I whisper all the time to Kyla, asking directions. She's sweating buckets, eyes wide in horror like the sockets can no longer hold them. But she keeps pointing, keeps directing. I just want to take her away from all this but in honesty, I wouldn't know where to go to leave.

We're not much of team considering how we came into this maelstrom but I feel better having the Sister here. She follows Kyla's lead past a molten lake and towards a large rocky crag. There's a path twisting up the side and as I look to the top I can see a figure surveying out over the scene before it. I've seen it before and I know it holds my love in its grasp.

"Up there, Sister. Do you see?"

"Do I see? Still the joke maker." I look over to see a smiling face from the nun. "Trimble, keep the dagger close. Any chance, you take it, any! Do you understand me? Let nothing stop you, nothing. We will all see things we don't want to see as we get close to it. It is a master of tricks, a master of lies. Do not fall for it. The only thing that matters is the corporeal destruction of that thing up there. Returning is not important, only success."

Chapter 44

Kyla's in agony and she writhes in my arms as I carry her along the track up the side of the rocky outcrop. It's hard to watch her face, a mix of horror and a straight forward pain but every now and then her body clutches up tight and I am forced to see if she has worsened. We don't need her directions anymore but I can't simply leave her lying around here with who knows what coming for her.

Sister Martha is at the front of our small pack with Hughes bringing up the rear. The tall Sergeant is looking very grim faced and has dried, caked blood around her nose and her temple but I know that won't stop her. No doubt thoughts of her children are keeping her going and she is in here until we finish this. Never in a million years did I think we would end up fighting these sort of creatures together when we started on the beat all those years ago.

The path is gravelly but also dusty and my shoes are picking up claggy grime. The heat is almost unbearable especially as I'm carrying Kyla and I start to sway under the intense sauna-like atmosphere. There's also raw fire in the near distance. And then there's nothing. Just nothing.

I spin round looking for something but can see nothing. Kyla's no longer in my arms. Instead I see them covered in blood and a voice laughs mocking me, saying that before me is my legacy for while it will have the city, I will have nothing. Shaking my head, I stand up, trying to appear defiant, shouting out to the void that it is far from over yet. I continue to stand as a silence renews. Nothing. Simply nothing around me.

With nothing to do, my mind starts to wander back to where it all started, not with the cup but with the first madness, the killings and the bombs. I drift off to that first meeting with Kyla at the train station, fighting for a happier memory but as soon as she comes into sight in my head there's a sudden light that blinds me.

And then I'm in Sketch's rooms, the front room specifically but I can hear something going on in the background. Sketch's voice is telling some unfortunate female how to pose, what to move and then giving a confirmatory "sexy". For lack of anything else to do, I wander on through to his rear studio and my eyes receive a shock. Kyla's dressed in a warrior outfit, one that wouldn't be very practical in battle or indeed even as a bikini. She's smiling, enjoying Sketch's attention.

When she notices me, she simply smiles and says "He does a good likeness." I cough and turn away but the room is filled with various portraits and drawings of Kyla in compromising positions and outfits and I turn to plant one on Sketch. But then it dawns on me. This is wrong. This is not what is.

"Liar," I shout. "This would never be her, she'd beat him to a pulp." And I think of her anger to Louis in the tunnel and how she felt he got his desserts. No, Kyla would never be like this.

"I can make her like this for you," says a voice, and I know it's the demon.

"No you can't. She has her own will."

"But it's what you'd like. What you would want."

I shake my head furiously. "Never. You can't force people to be what they don't want to be. She's no slave."

"I can."

"Bullshit," I cry, "and I wouldn't want her like that." And a voice says in my head *not unless she wanted to*. I can't believe where my mind goes at a time like this.

"Then maybe you should have what you really miss. What you really screwed up."

There's a blinding flash and I'm standing in a corridor. On either side are two apartments. I know this because I know the apartment block I'm standing in. Walking forward, I reach number 645 and knock on the door.

The door opens and a smiling blonde looks at me. "Come in, Mulgrew," she says.

"It's Kyle I say." And I gaze on the figure of Jenny Tatler, prior to the incident. She turns and I follow her swaying figure in a tight skirt she effortlessly moves about in. There's a table set for two and looking down at my hands I see a bottle of red and another of white.

Jenny is stirring something in a pot and I can smell the basil in the air. She was always a great cook, something of a hobby of hers. Standing at the table, I watch her figure dancing at the stove as a subtle little number plays on her music system. Yeah, I remember this time.

And then there's another snap of light and I'm standing on Jenny's balcony, her in front of me, the night air closing in. The chill is offset by the excitement between us and as I hold her from behind I feel her move with me and we dance slowly, intimately. Then my hand reaches for a zipper at the back of her top and…

We are suddenly on a soft chair, on the balcony, duvet around us watching the sun rise. Her face is peaceful as she sleeps in my arms and I remember the feeling I had right there, like the world was at ease, nothing was out of place and I wasn't going to get up ever.

"And here you can stay. Here with Jenny, before you destroyed her, before she fought her hatred of you to try and forgive. Leave your guilt behind and live right here in this moment. Renounce any other loves for this and I'll grant it to you forever."

My hand tussles Jenny's hair and her eyes open briefly looking at me like she used to, in wonder and joy. Dear God, she is perfect, this is…, is this even better than Kyla? I'd forgotten how strong I felt for her. But in the back of my mind, sits a different Jenny Tatler. A Jenny that told me not to mess it up with Kyla like I did with her, a woman who despite all the pain I caused her, still wants the best for me, still looks on me as a friend. Despite her troubles, despite the physical damage done to her Jenny is more beautiful now that even this moment before me.

"No. She's more than this. I'd live with the pain again to see what she's become. More than you could ever understand, could ever be."

I fall to the floor, all furnishings gone, and land on hot, clay-like soil. Standing up, I see before me two women. Jenny is there motionless, her head a mass of blood and her single arm broken to an impossible angle. Lying across her, also motionless is Kyla. Her hair is matted with a red stain and her legs are twisted into a wrong angle.

"This is your legacy, this is what you'll get for challenging me. But not before I've had my way with your whore. Not until I've taken both of them from you."

"You won't last this," I shout, unaware of how I'm even going to leave this scene never mind defeat this creature.

"Lasting was never the goal. Domination was never the goal. Don't you understand? Bedlam, it's not an achievement, it's a form of chaos. The utter and wanton destruction of all that is good and holy, the twisting of every decent thought and action. When I am done, you may stand but this city will have enough anger and hatred to carry out its own destruction without me."

And there's another flash. Kyla's in my arms and turning my head I see Hughes behind me with the same determined look on her face. Sister Martha turns from in front of me and stares with her lack of eyes and I think she's seeing inside me.

"Good Trimble, good. He doesn't have you. I thought you would get this the worst. But you are still standing. Good."

I nod but there's something in the back of my head, trying to knock on the door and get my attention. It's starting as a little tap and now it's causing a full on bludgeoning. And then it hits me. It showed me two bodies. Two broken women, two loves in my life.

"Martha, it's going for Jenny Tatler. It's going to kill Jenny Tatler."

Chapter 45

"That is irrelevant, Trimble, totally unimportant. Remember, first thing is to kill the corporeal form of that demon. There is nothing else." Sister Martha gives me an eyeless stare to make sure I understand. Easy for her, Jenny was never her lover, she doesn't feel she owes a debt to this woman.

The nun turns and starts to walk back up the path. Before us seems to be a clear path but with the number of attacks by things I can't even describe, I am more than wary. Kyla continues to moan in my arms, her eyes occasionally opening and I see the eyeballs swim before me. I feel so helpless with the situation, and I am hampered from any real reactionary movement by her. But it is better for Sister Martha to be free to deal with any attack for I have seen her in action.

"Up ahead," says Hughes, pointing out two figures coming back down the track towards us. I see what looks like the remembrance of men, large, six foot at least. But the figures are wispy, smoke forming features and I can almost see through them. There's a cautionary hand behind Sister Martha and she starts to say something under her breath. But she never stops walking forward.

As the figures draw close, one starts to dissipate and become a gaseous form coming towards Martha. It wraps itself around her and picks her up in some sort of binding and I wait for her response. But she doesn't flinch. Even as she is turned upside down. Hughes steps past me and throws a punch at the other form but finds her fist swinging clean through the form. The figure itself then swings an arm and slams Hughes into the rock face at the side of the path. I set Kyla down and make for the second figure reaching for the dagger up my back.

"No," says Martha, "Wait! I will deal with this."

I know better than to ignore this frail woman and I step back trying to provide a protective cover for Kyla. Glancing at Hughes, I see her shaking her head, blood running from a cut in the side of her head. Although groggy, she's breathing well.

"Nothings, you send me mere nothings. You insult me, demon. I will simply eat your pets."

I'm bemused at this rhetoric as Sister Martha is usually only ever cryptic, not outright weird. But she opens her mouth and starts to breathe in slowly. The smoke creature begins to be ingested by the nun and I believe I see the smoke strain as it begins to be drawn into Martha's mouth and nose. Slowly, it thins and I can see more of Martha through it with every passing second.

"What the hell?" says Hughes.

"Definitely not hell," I reply, giving Hughes a grin.

The first smoke creature has half disappeared into Sister Martha and I see her reach out a hand for the second one. She is a good four feet from the creature but there's already a force drawing it towards her. I swear there's panic on the face of the creature and it begins to draw out. The pace of consumption is increasing now and there's the sound of a fast wind coming from the Sister. And then with an incredible sucking sound the creatures race into Martha's mouth. She remains upside down in mid-air and her face is one of concentration. Slowly her body re-orientates and she lightly touches the ground.

"Way to go…" I start but she holds a finger up to her mouth seeking my silence. And then she turns to the rock face at the side of the path, gently waving Hughes out of the way. The nun braces her shoulders and then blows hard against the rock face, the smoke creatures being ejected and reforming against the wall. But they are held there by a wind from Martha's mouth. And then I turn as a bright white fire or maybe a light comes from her mouth. I throw my hands up but I am still blinded temporarily before I begin to see some spots and then a full picture.

There's simply nothing at the rock face. Martha stands looking a little out of breath but otherwise perfectly well. Quickly, I scan the area but the creatures are gone.

"How on earth..?" I ask.

"Pets, Detective Trimble, mere pets."

The sister walks on and I grab Kyla who seems to have passed out. As she's seemingly out cold, I put her over my shoulder as the path seems to be growing steeper. Hughes has gathered herself but still seems somewhat disorientated. I use my other hand to help steer her and I begin to feel like we are just the army's escort wagon of food and washer women from the 18th Century, Martha being the main force of men in uniform.

As we continue on, Martha keeps turning her head to the side as if listening for something. There's a flap of wings from above and I see her begin to smile. "I've been waiting for this one, Trimble, waiting a long time. Just keep going and I'll be back, Detective. Only be a short while but this one is personal."

I don't understand what she is on about but am too occupied

with Hughes and Kyla to worry about it. Then comes a screech from above, but with infernal overtones. It sounds like a bird until you realize that no bird ever called with such evil intonations. I drop to my knees, pulling Hughes down with my spare hand.

But Martha simply stands there and I watch as two large claws dig into her shoulders and she is lifted off her feet and into the air. It's a leathery creature, all in black and I fail to see the face as it flies off with its catch. Martha doesn't seem to be struggling despite the fact that the claws went straight into her shoulders.

My heart sinks as she is flown off into the distance. But she anticipated it, almost welcomed it. And she said to go on. To continue. So I tap Hughes on the shoulder and indicate we move forward. Her face is full of fear. Like me, she's seeing things she cannot believe, and our leader has just disappeared, clawed away from us. But I see the same determination that's always there.

Together we walk on, almost belligerently, as if not to would be a sin. Maybe it would, maybe not to fight is a sin. I don't know anymore, I am clinging on to my orders, my instructions for Martha, trusting she knows about these things. Kyla suddenly starts banging with her fist on my back and I drop her to her feet. She's awoken and looks a mess, hands protectively covering her body despite being fully clothed.

"He's right here," she says to me, eyes wide and full of fear. "Kyle, get him off me, dear God Kyle get him off me."

And with that she is suddenly pulled away from me, her heels dragging while she remains upright held by some invisible force, and disappears up the path. As she rounds the corner, all I have left are the long lines her heels have dug into the grimy dust.

Looking at Hughes, I get a nod and I prepare for what will be the final effort. "You are one proper mother," I say. She laughs. It feels like the strongest kick we can give to the enemy at the moment.

Chapter 46

I seem somewhat more upbeat than I should be but when things get this bad, what can you do? You can get depressed by it all but that helps no one. Or you can laugh inappropriately and pretend it's not as bad as all that and get on with it. I choose the latter because the other is not my style. You have no idea how many really awful situations I have got through by pretending they are nothing.

Hughes walks on beside me wondering what's going on around the next corner. After all that we've seen so far I'm not expecting to be surprised. But never say never. There's a part of me that's trembling inside though. Our Joker in the pack is gone, Sister Martha taken away and it seemed without the merest fight. It wasn't like her.

I contemplate the weapons we have and except for the dagger up my back, we have nothing. Sister Martha said the demon cannot see the dagger but if it's in full view his minions might and that's why it has to stay as hidden as possible. Still, the thought of just having my fists and feet as a defense isn't filling me with the greatest hope. Hughes has bigger fists and a meaner punch so she's alright. There's that inappropriate laugh again.

There's a scurrying sound from up ahead now and I look

for where it is coming from but there's nothing. The sound is incessant now and getting louder. And it's sounding like it's from beneath my feet.

An explosion of grimy soil later and I'm up in the air hanging upside down with a screaming pain in my leg. Something has my limb and is swinging me about from it. I try to grab it with my hands but it's so slimy that they simply slip off it. Hughes is battering it with her fists and maybe it's doing some damage. Time for another inappropriate laugh. Not so easy when you're upside down and being flung around.

"Put him down! The master wants him." The voice is efficient and like an old style butler. As the shaking stops suddenly, I manage to catch a glimpse of an elderly looking man who has the gauntest face I have ever seen. His cheek bones ride up like they are about to burst the skin and if he came to any hospital they would rush him into the accident and emergency department.

The creature drops me and I fall head first, managing to get my arms out and perform a largely ineffective roll. Hughes helps me up and together we stare at this new individual who stares intently at us.

"Where is the older lady? Where is the nun? He has asked for the nun." The voice is gravelly with age but has a slickness to it, perfect intonation and a feeling of service.

"Don't look at me. Your worm thing was throwing me about. Some winged creature took the Sister."

"Blast it, sir, you give such bad news. The Master wanted you and the nun. As for your companion I guess I shall bring her as well. He didn't ask but no doubt he will want her if I don't bring her along. Come along then, we don't want to be late."

"Whoa!" I shout, "Just a damn minute. Who are you and why should we go with you? I ain't here for dinner, I'm here to end all this. And why the pleasant *please follow me*. I've fought plenty of your blasted creatures up till now. Lost some good, and some not so good people." I'm thinking of Louis. "What's this shenanigans after the battle?"

"I do not question the Master. He commands I retrieve you and so I retrieve you. Now come along."

"No. I'll go on my own terms." I stand defiant with Hughes showing a grimace beside me daring the butler figure to move her.

"There is no need for this. If you'll just proceed in an orderly fashion, we'll be there in no time. Maybe he's got an offer for you, sir. He's prone to generosity."

"I've had his offers and frankly, no."

"As you wish." The man seems to sigh and bows his head. From behind him a pair of dark wings erupt and then flap before settling down into a sort of large ruff around his back. The head lifts and he smiles, his canine teeth now pronounced and showing as large fangs. "It has been three hundred years of service and I have never failed to bring my Master whatever he has requested."

"There's always a first time."

The man looks straight at Hughes, his eyes seemingly boring at her. I fear what's happening and start to run at the man but he holds up a hand. My feet scrape the dust on the ground as I try to propel myself forward but it's like there's a glass wall in front of me.

"Come my dear." Hughes walks directly forward following the man. "I guess you'll follow her. There's no need to fear, rather accept your fate and all shall go smoothly. I fear he may not give you another offer, his generosity often wanes if he is refused."

I feel the air in front of me relent as the man walks off with Hughes following behind like a lamb. "If I'm invited to meet him, what's his name?"

"You would not understand the name, sir, for it is in their language, that of hell itself. However, you would know him in your tongue as *The Darkness*. You met his envoy. The Master was not pleased at his failure. But you impressed with your foiling of his plans. But not just you, your wench as well. That is why he wants her. To show you that he is in charge, his will, will be done."

"I always thought it was God's will be done. A good catholic boy, myself."

"Don't make such rash claims. There's plenty evil in you to come to the Master's side. Follow me now and learn the power of my Master and you may yet beg for your life and more. Enter the servitude and become a useful tool again and enjoy the rewards. I dare say you could have your blonde wench again."

What truly hacks me off is how my previous love life is coming back as common knowledge. I'd gotten over it, made peace that Jenny was a good friend and just that. Now everyone wants to put us back together again. And not for good reasons. Don't see Jenny taking that.

"Lead on then, I'll see your boss but he needs to be aware he may not like me. My mom always said I was too sarcastic for my own good." I trudge after the figure who seems to have ignored my last comment. The thought of a face to face with this demon isn't making me feel good but I knew it was coming. After all, this was the mission, to find and kill him. But with

Kyla captured ahead, Hughes under control and Sister Martha somewhere else in the claws of something bad, it isn't looking good.

Still, put on a happy face, isn't that what they say.

Chapter 47

There's a weary trudge to my feet as I walk forward to the inevitable showdown with the demon. Last night I didn't do so well and it seems like a futile effort, especially with the only person who really knows what they are doing on this side, Sister Martha, having been taken away by some creature. But Kyla's also up ahead and I need to bring her back, back to something normal, something other than this madness. It seems a long time since she sat on the bench in my arms waiting for a taxi. That moment seems quite special now.

The butler, as I call him, leads on with loping strides. Hughes doesn't utter a word, her eyes still glazed over, her strong form now a figure of drooping shoulders and defeat. But I still have my knife, unseen, unknown. Though how to get close to use it, I don't know.

The path up the rocky outcrop gets gradually steeper, forcing me to put my hands on my knees. There are a few creatures lining the path, some in a shadow form, others, Serpentine or rat-like in form. I can't help but shake my head at it all. This is madness.

As we reach a crest in the path, the butler turns to Hughes and tells her to "make sure he stays here", before walking over the crest. Turning to me, but with eyes still glazed, Hughes grips my arms tightly. I don't struggle. There's enough coming without taking on a friend. Still her grip is something to behold, it feels like the circulation is going to stop in my arm.

The butler returns and he stares at me. "The Master will see you now. He has a few other guests you may be acquainted with."

It looks like I may be too late for Jenny Tatler but if she's there I might have a chance. I reckon the more good bodies in the building the higher the odds I can beat this impossible challenge. And if I don't well, we gave it a go. Not that this delightful sentiment in any way stops me from feeling like I'm about to enter a living hell. I sweat profusely as we walk along and I undo the shirt by a few buttons. With a medallion, I'd look like a real stud. If only.

As I crest the top of the ridge, I see the demon, the horns and bizarre animal concoction that it is. It's got its back to me and I'm good with that but what is disturbing is how Kyla seems to be floating beside him, wrapped up in a curled ball, almost smiling to herself and making slight groaning noises. A further scan lets me see Jenny Tatler tied to a tree by her hand. She's bloodied and her skirt is ripped, her shirt bedraggled and I can feel the rage rising. She's chained like a dog.

"Quite the catch and she's yours if you want her. Not a bad prize when you can't have exactly what you want. Although the brunette is friskier. Harder to beat into shape, to break to one's will. But she will bend to it."

There's a hollow part in my stomach that wants to rise to the top and be sick. I'm a man like any other but the demon knows how to humiliate women. They are the kind of words that would go straight to Kyla's gut, cause her to fight back hard. I see her start to twitch and break out of her contented ball. But the demon reaches out and smacks her head with his hand.

"No you don't. You do as told, wench." That's another blow to her psyche. But the physical strike must have been stronger than it looked because she immediately snaps back into her ball.

"I'm somewhat disappointed," I say, "I thought someone like yourself would have had a bit more of a greater agenda. You simply want to own these women. There's plenty of men who have similar desires to your own."

"Fool, I don't want to own them sexually, I want to own them. Take their soul as my plaything as well as their body. And I want yours too, Trimble. My servant may want your body but I will own you in all that you do. I will take this world and be the Master of it. Of everything, right to your pitiful and empty core."

"Can't allow that. You see this is my city." My voice is weak but I keep going with the speech as I don't know quite what else to do. It's too far away for an attack. "And we have laws, you cannot just walk in and take the place. You got to pay taxes for a start, unless you find one of the more corrupt members of town hall staff…"

"Be quiet. You're not here for the petty banter. You're here to show the world what commitment is. When you drink the potion you'll soon dispatch your beloved woman, right before the eyes of the world. A fallen hero. Always good for showing the masses."

"That won't be happening," I say quietly.

"Oh it will. I wanted it to be the nun, you killing a poor blind nun, the public will love it and it would cripple you forever.

This will too. But enough talk, it is time for you to accept your fate. Come here and put your arm out."

I try to turn but there's Hughes holding my arm again like it is the most valuable thing on earth. Maybe it is, Jenny might say that. Hughes drags me over towards the demon who materializes a seat and table out of thin air.

"I think you'll know my latest employee. Does some rather good work in tattoos."

Sketch is suddenly sitting at the table, looking very perplexed and then on seeing the demon, very scared. He looks at me with petrified eyes and makes promises that he is being forced to do this. My arm is taken and stretched out allowing Sketch to get to work with his sharp tools and I bite down on my teeth as he draws.

Looking at my arm, I see the figure emerge and it shows Kyla lying in a revealing pose, devoid of clothing, with warrior bracelets and ankle bands. She brandishes a sword too. I'm swooning from the heat but it actually does look great.

"And now, Trimble, you will partake of the cup and then hunt down your beloved. Don't worry I'll save the blonde for you."

"But you wanted her, you wanted Kyla, and she'll be dead." I'm very desperate now. The whole thing makes no sense to me but then again it's my first demon.

"I can have her in many more ways than you can ever imagine. Anyway I will tire of her soon."

I won't but I've got Hughes now grabbing me and lifting my arm up so that I am dragged across to a small altar. She picks me up and places me on my back with little effort. From the corner of my eye, I see a figure holding the cup and letting the blood from it fall down her habit, lying open at the front.

Hughes' hand is like a clamp on my chest and I cannot move. The redhead now walks toward me, her habit hiding little and the blood spilling from the cup. I struggle now, kicking out my legs but to no available. Hughes has me laid down tight. The redhead tips the cup over my mouth and I blow out hard, forcing the liquid away from my mouth.

"Bloody hold him," cries the redhead and tries again. This time Hughes has my mouth held open. This time there's no avoiding the liquid.

Chapter 48

I've tasted blood in my mouth before but not someone else's. The cup continues to tip and the red liquid flows into my mouth, causing me to choke as I try to spit it out. Above me is the figure of the redhead, grinning and delighting in my struggle. As the blood flows down my throat, I feel like there's a fire running toward my stomach. I begin to twist and yell, and all around suddenly grows into a veiled theater, like a grey mist has descended on it.

One figure stands out from this cover, that of the redhead, her curves and scant clothing firing my inner base nature. I reach up for her and she playfully taps my hands away, pointing to the distance. There's now no hands on my stomach and I turn over to see only one other person in the fog. She's curled in a ball but is starting to unravel herself.

It's like every piece of hatred I have ever felt has rushed to the fore of my mind and is screaming at me to rip this person apart. In the depths, there's a voice, a quiet but constant voice that says I know this person, that I want this person, not to rip them apart. But there's also a hundred voices screaming at me to do it.

A hand is placed on my neck and I turn my head to see the redhead, stroking the back of my hair, like I'm some sort of dog. I'm currently on all fours so the analogy holds. Despite the core instinct I have not to be anyone's pet, I am submissive to her touch. She kisses my face, long and slow, clearly to tease the person before us. A wet tongue lashes across my cheeks, ear and then my neck.

"Kill her for me. Bring me back a body to feast on."

I snarl like a dog, looking at the redhead's revealed figure, girded by her near nakedness. Lust races to the fore as I now focus on the other figure which stands with a hand out before it, imploring me to stay back.

"No, Kyle, You don't know what you're doing. Stop Kyle. Dear God, just stop."

They are just words from someone, not a non-entity but someone unknown to me, a piece of filth to remove. It's like my whole essence has become the removal of this person. I run forward, arms outstretched to grab them. There's a kick to my side and then a punch to my head but there's no feeling of pain. I grab the person's throat, holding them before me. A scream from them is choked out and I turn as I hear the redhead encourage me on.

"Good, hold her for a moment. Let the camera record your destruction of this wench."

Looking around but maintaining my throttling grip, I see the demon, I feel the hate and anger coursing from it into me. Fueling me. I grin at it as my choke becomes more intense. There's another voice now. A woman's voice and a feeling somewhere that I know it. But I also don't care.

"Don't Trimble. Look at me, Mulgrew, look at me. This isn't you. Don't bloody do it. No Kyle!"

"How they beg," says the demon but I'm unsure exactly what it is referring to, my hands continuing its throttle. "Let the one armed one off her leash. See if she can stop him or perish. Give her the big woman too. Let them all struggle."

Something hits me on the back but I don't register if it's a hard or light blow. There's simply no sensation except the acknowledgement that something struck me. I swing my free arm but catch nothing and then receive blows to my midriff. Someone else is now close to my face screaming, waving a single arm at me.

"Trimble!"

I turn and see the redhead and I subconsciously lick my lips. She's flaunting herself at me and despite receiving constant blows I watch her, relishing her vulgarity.

"Finish her! Finish her and have me, Trimble."

Turning back to the figure I am holding, I increase the pressure on the neck. With my free hand, I swipe at and knock the one armed person away from me. The other person who was raining down blows now grabs my throat but I feel nothing, except the raw charge of hatred and anger that makes me feel like I could snap a neck without even thinking.

Then there's a hand on my head and someone is whispering out something akin to a prayer. It might be Latin, Italian or some other language but it is being spoken at pace and by someone who seems to be a native to the tongue. Swinging my head I look for the person and then see a face with no eyes.

"I will take it Trimble, I will take it from you. All the hate, the anger, let me have it."

I don't want to, I want to keep it, to use it to strangle the life out of this person before me, to languish in my lust for this redhead. But I feel it being drawn from me, I feel the hate being stripped away. I throw a punch out at one of the grabbing figures and feel it connect with a jaw. But the eyeless face remains, determined.

And then the figure in my hand becomes clearer. The hair that is still tied up behind that neck. I'd recognize it anywhere. The face turning blue now and seemingly with little life. The figure I have hungered for, have admired, have even tried to love in my own way that hangs limp before me. My hand opens and Kyla drops from my grasp.

I slowly look around and see Jenny Tatler lying on the floor, blood streaming from her mouth, her lower jaw offset to where its normal location would be. Behind me, there's a groan and on looking I see a tall powerhouse of a policewoman, her face bruised but with a smile. And then I look into the face of Sister Martha.

She is contorted as if in battle with something. I step back as she starts to thrash about, obviously struggling to control what she has taken from me. I step forward but she throws out a straight arm knocking me off my feet as she continues to try to contain the rage within. I understand her, understand what she's going through.

"Well done, Detective," laughs the Demon, "She was pure, hard to break down, to tempt, to weaken but now you have put an evil, a rage, an anger that will break her. That will bring her to me. Well done, Detective, very well done."

I look around and see the redhead laughing. My heart sinks as Sister Martha continues to thrash about in obvious pain. I look at my battered colleagues and then I look on the floor. Kyla has still not moved. Her throat still has the marks from my hands on it. I don't know if I've killed her. I don't know if she's breathing.

Chapter 49

"That's it, His bride, His own daughter, come to me." The demon laughs as Sister Martha, bubbling like an over boiled cauldron, struggles but fails to ignore the creature's beckoning. Step by step, her contorted body makes its way over to the horned being and I feel powerless to stop it. My own heart is sunk, seeing Kyla lying on the floor.

But then I hear Jenny Tatler swear and get back to her feet, her jaw hanging awkwardly. "No you don't," she spits, and stumbles forward toward the demon. But she is intercepted by a flash of skin and a monk's habit. There's a flash of nails and Jenny hits the floor with long raking marks across her face, blood dripping from them.

I'm paralyzed by what I have done to Kyla, stood like a useless statue, gawping at all around me. Hughes rushes past and plants a right hook any boxer would have been proud of on the redhead who falls under the blow. But any further progress is stopped as the demon holds up a hand and Hughes goes into the trance state she was in when being brought to the rocky outcrop.

I have Kyla's head in my hands now and I'm not sure she is breathing. My eyes wander from the enchanting face I've possibly killed to the grotesque scene unfolding before me.

Sister Martha is now floating a few inches off the ground at the demons beckoning and it's mocking her figure. "Worn out hag, not even good for a bad time."

Martha's face is emotionless as the demon casually walks on its hooves to the edge of the outcrop, Martha floating alongside. It stands on the very edge and lets Martha float right in front of itself, facing it. Her face is drawn close and the demon spits a fiery breath onto her eyes.

"Maybe I should heal your vision so you can see the destruction you have brought on people by your failure. Where is your God now, Sister? Where was He when your friend, the father, died, when you failed to protect him? When he died cursing your name, where, Sister, tell me where? I will suck every inch of morsel of faith from you before I drop your carcass onto the ground below to feed my creatures of the dark."

"No!" I shout. "Let her go."

"Silence," cries the demon and I feel my lips being forced together. I try to get up but it's like an enormous stone has been placed on my lap and I cannot move. The redhead comes over to me and stands behind me, curving a leg round my body. I feel the press of her from behind, trying to stimulate my body with every touch, even as I have Kyla in my arms. The woman spits and I see the saliva on Kyla's cheek but I can't move to wipe it clean. A hand roams my chest and my skin begins to crawl.

Jenny Tatler is lying face down after the punishment she received but she manages to look in my direction. She's winking an eye at me and I know what it means. Jenny's going to try something, I don't know what but she's waiting for her moment. I don't know what she can do, it's all so hopeless.

Martha is still thrashing about as she hangs in mid-air before the demon. It's insulting her body, physically now as well as verbally. I can feel the tears of hopelessness running down my cheeks.

"Relax, Detective, once he kills the bitch Sister, I can finish off your own cow and then you'll have me. We can romp as the city burns. You'll be in heaven with me, the real one, the only one that matters."

Her hand snakes over me again but I am so cold inside I don't even feel her attempts to arouse me. Looking at Martha, I feel the despair setting in. She was the one who was supposed to know what to do, the one with a plan. All this craziness was her world, not mine. She knew how to beat the demon. I knew she knew. She must have known, so why save me, why not simply let me go and take the demon on without warning? Looking at her now, I see only failure.

And then the demon reaches forward with one of its hands and it seems to go inside Sister Martha. Form the position of the arm, it looks like the demon has just reached up inside Martha and grabbed her heart. She screams. It's loud and grows and the demon seems to delight in squeezing harder.

And then Martha throws her body forward, wrapping her arms around the demon while its own hand is still inside her. She cries out in Latin, or Italian, whatever it is and I see the demon's face draw back in horror. It tries to shake her off but she's locked tight to it.

"Trimble, now! Do it now!"

I try to throw off the redhead from my back but her arms and legs are wrapped around me and I can't get up. But then Jenny Tattler's there, swinging her one arm into the face of the redhead, cutting hard and drawing blood.

Feeling the redhead's hold weaken, I bite an arm and am

released. Then I push up with my feet shrugging her off my back and letting Kyla drop to the floor.

"Hurry Trimble, I can't hold it for long," shouts the Sister, whose heart is still being squeezed. I reach up my back and pull out the dagger, the one Martha gave me so long ago. The demon looks at me but it's like he doesn't see the dagger, just me running forward.

"Halt," it cries.

The air becomes suddenly thick and it's like I'm walking through treacle. I can barely move but I keep pushing as I hear Martha chanting again. There's a sudden release and I stumble before the force is back, but not as strong as before. It seems like an age and I can hear fighting behind me, but I manage to make my way over.

Martha's hands are clamped together and the demon is now on fire, the flames licking Martha's skin, burning her features. Part of her face is blackened with burns. Her clothes are burning too and she still has her feet just over the edge of the outcrop.

"Get clear," I shout to Martha.

"No! If I let go, it'll control you."

"But I'll stab you as well."

"Do it! Nothing I said, nothing is more important."

Some people will say my lack of a pause is a sign of a lack of compassion. But I am a cop and we need to get things done so I obey the Sister. Driving the knife up into the back of the demon, it goes clean though and slices into Martha. She yells but her grip is remorseless.

The demon rages as I stab it again, and again. And then the combined figure of Sister Martha and the demon topples forward off the outcrop, falling several hundred meters to the ground. My hand now trembles. Stepping gingerly forward I look down to see only one body, that of Sister Martha. There's blood from her head and her limbs are at awkward angles.

But there's no demon, and no dusty path below. It's a pavement and as I look at my feet, I am standing on the roof of a tall building.

I think we won.

Chapter 50

They said to get away, to get some space from it all. Well, that was easier said than done. Even after all the press intrusion, the department and local government briefings, and then the actual clean-up operation, there were all the funerals. I can't remember how many times I stood silently as they lowered another colleague or friend into the ground. The battle in the demon's world was weird and intense but the battle in the city was also bloody and brutal.

Many we buried I had walked the beat with many years ago. And they did what I knew they would do, give it all to protect the public. The authorities put it down to a fancy drug causing mass hysteria and giving enormous temporary strength and madness to individuals. They also said there may have been a cult element to it, possibly Satanic in nature. That was as far as they were prepared to go.

Martha's funeral was the hardest. I still think there must have been another way but I don't see it. I carried her coffin, along with Hughes and a few of her people from the cathedral. Unlike them, I could feel every stab I made with each step I took. I still don't know how I held it together.

Kobold and Gonzales made it. She has a broken leg to mend and he took a deep cut to his back but was otherwise unharmed.

Well, physically at least. Mentally I doubt we'll ever recover. As for the rest of the team who stepped across into that hell, we never saw them again.

Jenny Tatler spent quite a while in hospital. Every other evening I went up and sat by her bed to talk to her. She said little but then again her jaw needed to be reset after being broke, so I felt I had to talk to make up for it. Her face has scar lines across it, long and raking. The doctor says they will heal but the lines won't go away.

During the whole time I was there, I think apart from anyone from the department, I saw only one other visitor. That was her sister and she doesn't like me as I broke Jenny's heart in the past. But I was needed. On my third visit, Jenny broke down and I climbed onto the bed and held her as she wept. It's just mental trauma, they said. When was such trauma ever a *just*?

And Kyla? Yeah, I have been remiss in mentioning her, haven't I? That's because it's kinda of hard to talk about. I mean I throttled her. Properly throttled her. The good news I guess is that I didn't kill her.

She's lying beside me now on a sun bed, and she may actually be asleep. The sun's getting weaker now but it's still covering her body, tanning the skin that the bikini doesn't cover. In truth, she's breathtaking to behold, I think any man knows that feeling as he looks on his love. But the road has been rough.

She spent time in hospital and every day I saw those deep purple marks on her neck. There were nightmares that would cause her to thrash about in her sleep and then she would awake and see the face that had caused her this pain – mine.

With everything else that was going in the wake of what happened I guess we just put ourselves on hold. We'd go out to some little restaurant or coffee house but we literally ate or drank. I mean how do you even begin to start to talk about this stuff?

And then we tried the other method of communicating but whatever that thing did to her, it cut her to the core. When I touched her she would panic, curl up and shake. I think it was easier when she was paralyzed. We tried some therapy too but I'm awful at that sort of thing and in honesty, Kyla is as well. Cops you see, we can play the poker face too well. No one gets in when they pry either.

That was when I called it, three weeks away, remote island, just the two of us, or as near as I could afford. We have accommodation and it's gone pretty well. Apart from the guy who showed us the place we haven't seen anyone. And we've talked. Not enough but we have. And the other stuff. Yeah some of that but that's taking a lot more time for obvious reasons. But the right direction. Definitely the right direction.

Kyla gets up beside me and takes a hair tie tying her brunette mane up behind her neck in a ponytail. There's the neck that sold me, still dark purple in color. Surely the bruises will leave sometime.

"Tonight, let's midnight swim. Let's make it fun, Kyle, see if that helps."

I nod. "Of course but it wasn't exactly warm when the sun went down. And the breeze is picking up."

"So what? We go for a dip in our coats? I think the only thing we should take is a bottle of something nice."

"You serious?"

Kyla smiles wickedly. And then I see the hesitation. "I want to try. Let's give it a go. I'll go make the dinner now, it's my turn before you offer to do it. You go stretch your legs for a bit.

You've been sat there gawping at me for the last three hours, you could do with a walk."

Standing up I salute. "Yes, Ma'am." For my mockery, I get a punch to the arm, followed by a kiss.

"Go on, off you go."

Reckoning that she usually likes a good half hour to make dinner, I walk from our accommodation, which sits on a small inlet thus giving us a private beach, to the cliff lines beside it. The view's quite delightful with the sun slowly setting and the surf rolling gently in. There's a light breeze which may make tonight cold but I am not missing it for anything.

Standing at the cliff top, I breathe in deeply before taking a look at my tattoo. It caused such pain and I offered to take it off but Kyla said she'd ask if she needed it to go. Sketch is a heck of an artist and Kyla looks amazing in the image, albeit a pose and a choice of clothing that she's unlikely to ever need or use.

A flash of red on the beach. Something moved down there. I get closer to the edge and look down. Sure enough, there's a person wrapped in red with a hood on as well. As I watch my mind clocks the size and shape. It can't be. I should have said but I don't talk about her since the incident. We never found the redhead's body amongst the devastation in Edelweiss. No sign or trace of her.

But now I think she may be on the beach below. Looking around, I see an awkward but useable path down the cliff and start to scramble my way down. After some significant drops, I look again to see if the figure is still there. It is and looking right up at me.

A pair of hands drops the hood off the head and I see a tangle of red hair. The hands then travel to the opening of the clothing and I see the figure rip open what they are wearing at the front. The wind billows the clothing and I see the milky white flesh that chills me to the bone. Flaunting herself, she waves a beckoning hand at me.

I turn back to the rock and scramble down again but the next time I look over my shoulder she's gone. Dammit. Continuing down, I soon reach the sand and look around desperately. Footprints, there should be footprints. But there are none, except for my own. Did I dream her? Did my mind just decide to play a trick on me? My hands are clammy, I can feel myself sweating. I thought she was gone, she must be gone.

It must have been an illusion, a blip in my mind. She can't be here. How would she even know where to find us? I didn't tell anyone where we were going, not even Kyla. And there is nothing here. I breathe out a simple sigh but as I turn I see an envelope on the sand.

It's white and has my name on it, written in red. Actually, that looks like blood, and fairly fresh. I rip open the envelope and there's a single piece of paper with a very simple message:

Enjoy your bitch while she breathes, you will be mine!

About the Author

GR Jordan is a self-published author who finally decided at forty that in order to have an enjoyable lifestyle, his creative beast within would have to be unleashed. His books mirror that conflict in life where acts of decency contend with self-promotion, goodness stares in horror at evil and kindness blind-side us when we at our worst. Corrupting our world with his parade of wondrous and horrific characters, he highlights everyday tensions with fresh eyes whilst taking his methodical, intelligent mainstays on a roller-coaster ride of dilemmas, all the while suffering the banter of their provocative sidekicks.

A graduate of Loughborough University where he masqueraded as a chemical engineer but ultimately played American football, Gary had worked at changing the shape of cereal flakes and pulled a pallet truck for a living. Watching vegetables freeze at -40'C was another career highlight and he was also one of the Scottish Highlands "blind" air traffic controllers.

These days he has graduated to answering a telephone to people in trouble before telephoning other people to sort it out.

Having flirted with most places in the UK, he is now based in the Isle of Lewis in Scotland where his free time is spent between raising a young family with his wife, writing, figuring out how to work a loom and caring for a small flock of chickens. Luckily his writing is influenced by his varied work and life experience as the chickens have not been the poetical inspiration he had hoped for!

You can connect with me on:

🌐 https://grjordan.com

🐦 https://twitter.com/carpetless

📘 https://facebook.com/carpetlessleprechaun

Subscribe to my newsletter:

✉ https://mailchi.mp/bf149bd0218b/crescendo

Also by G R Jordan

G R Jordan writes across multiple genres including dark and action adventure fantasy, feel good fantasy, mystery thriller and horror fantasy. Below are a selection of his work grouped together in their genres, starting with the popular Austerley & Kirkgordon action adventure fantasy. Whilst all books are available across online stores, signed copies are available at his personal shop

The Blasphemous Welcome: Dark Wen Book 1

https://grjordan.com/product/the-blasphemous-welcome

A demonic entity prepares a bloody path for its master. Four fiendish ways for the city folk to die. A cynical, battle weary detective must become his home's heavenly protector.

Join Detective Trimble and fresh faced Kyla Corstain as they enter a world of evil and ungodly manipulation causing murder, mayhem and disaster. The war for a city's soul begins now!

The Dark Wen series opens with a fanfare of destruction and death raining upon a city held in the grip of an unknown force. If you like dark powers, fast paced action and a generous dose of occult warfare, then "The Blasphemous Welcome" will satisfy your story cravings.

Austerley & Kirgordon Adventures Box Set: Books 1-3 and Origin stories 1-3 (Austerley& Kirkgordon)
https://grjordan.com/product/ak-box-set

A retired bodyguard looking for a little fun before it's too late. An obsessive Professor, seeking the darkest things of life. And an Elder god seeking to rule the world, if they can't stop him.

Join Austerley and Kirkgordon on the rollercoaster ride that is their first three adventures. Comprising 3 full novels as well as three accompanying origin novelettes, this collection will introduce you to a polarised duo that are the world's best hope. With them for the adventure are a myriad of strange characters, bizarre animals, evil humans and the UK's finest agents from its most secret department.

As one reviewer put it, "If you like Lovecraft, Poe, or Conan Doyle you will like this book. If you like tv show like Buffy the Vampire Slayer, Supernatural, Being Human, or X-Files you will like this book."

So take a chance on a molotov cocktail of a duo and see how to save the world on the wild side.

Surface Tensions (Island Adventures Book 1)

https://grjordan.com/product/surface-tensions

Mermaids sighted near a Scottish island. A town exploding in anger and distrust. And Donald's got to get the sexiest fish in town, back in the water.

"Surface Tensions" is the first story in a series of Island adventures from the pen of G R Jordan. If you love comic moments, cosy adventures and light fantasy action, then you'll love these tales with a twist. Get the book that amazon readers said, "perfectly captures life in the Scottish Hebrides" and that explores "human nature at its best and worst".

Something's stirring the water!

Water's Edge: A Highlands and Islands Detective Thriller (Highlands & Islands Detective Book 1

https://grjordan.com/product/waters-edge

A body discovered by the rocks. A broken detective returns to a scene of past tragedy. Will the pain of the past prevent him from seeing the present?

Detective Inspector Macleod returns to his island home twenty years after the painful loss of his wife. With a disposition forged in strong religious conservatism, he must bond with his new partner, the free spirited and upcoming female star of the force, to seek the killer of a young woman and shine a light on the evil beneath the surface. To do so, he must once again stand in the place where he lost everything. Only at the water's edge, will everything be made new.

The rising tide brings all things to the surface.

www.ingramcontent.com/pod-product-compliance
Lightning Source LLC
Chambersburg PA
CBHW031007190726
48286CB00003BA/727